POUNDED IN THE PATCH

DARK NIGHTS COLLECTION

DANA LEEANN

POUNDED IN THE PATCH

DARK NIGHTS COLLECTION

DANA LEEANN

CONTENT WARNINGS

Pounded in the Patch is an erotic horror novella. The first 3/4 of this book will very much read as dubcon. Parts of it might even feel like noncon. If you are easily triggered by either of these things, I strongly recommend you do not continue with this book. Your mental health matters more than any book ever will. You are important.

Some of the heavy content within this book includes (but is not limited to): dubcon (noncon could also be argued), explicit language, explicit sexual content (there are like 9-10 orgasms in this little novella), primal play, kidnapping, bondage, restraints, knife play, blood, mention of drug use and being drugged, breath play/face fucking.

If you find something I haven't included in this list, but think it should be included, please reach out via email:

danaleeannauthor@gmail.com. I will get it added immediately. Mental health matters and I take content warnings very seriously.

A literary masterpiece?
No, baby. This is a spooky fucking ride.

For those who want their pumpkin spice with a side of being absolutely ruined by a masked man

CHAPTER 1
TAKEN

Seraphina

The rope burns against my wrists as consciousness creeps back in like a thief in the night, stealing away the merciful darkness that had been my refuge.

My eyes flutter open to beams of moonlight trickling in through a window above my head. The world sways beneath me with a bumpy motion that makes my stomach lurch violently—I'm in a moving vehicle. The back seat, I realize with growing horror, based on the black leather pressed against my cheek and the way my knees are bent at an awkward, painful angle that suggests I've been unconscious for quite some time.

What the fuck is happening?

Panic and bile rise in my throat as I try to move my arms, only to feel thick rope binding my wrists behind my back. The coarse fibers dig into my skin with every slight movement, sending sharp stings up my forearms that make me bite back a whimper. My ankles are tied too, I realize with mounting terror, as I attempt to straighten my legs and feel more rope cutting into the skin above my boots.

This can't be real. This *cannot* be real.

The steady rumble of the engine fills my ears, a monotonous drone that almost seems to vibrate through my bones. Mixed with it is the sound of tires on gravel— we're moving fast. My heart is racing so quickly I can feel my pulse pounding, each beat echoing through my ears like a war drum.

Think, Seraphina. Think. What's the last thing you remember?

I force myself to focus, to push past the panic and try to piece together how the fuck I ended up here. Memory comes in fragments, disjointed and hazy like trying to remember a dream.

I remember leaving work. The accounting firm's office building, with its millennial gray walls and fluorescent lighting that always makes everything look slightly sickly. I remember stepping outside into the autumn evening air, crisp and clean with that distinctive October bite. The scent of fallen leaves had filled my nostrils, mixed with the exhaust from evening traffic and something else...

I remember being excited about something. The weekend, maybe? I had plans, I think. Something I was looking forward to. But what?

Come on. Focus.

I was walking to my car in the parking garage. The click of my heels on the concrete, the way the sound echoed off the walls... I was reaching for my keys, digging through my purse with one hand while balancing my laptop bag and the stack of files I'm supposed to review over the weekend.

And then... nothing.

Nothing.

A complete blank, like someone has taken an eraser to my memory and wiped away everything that came after. The thought makes my skin crawl with unease.

How long have I been unconscious? Where am I? *Who* is driving this car?

The questions multiply in my mind, each one spawning new terrors. I try to slow my breathing, to think logically right now, but it's nearly impossible when every rational thought is drowned out by the screaming voice in my head that keeps repeating *kidnapped, kidnapped, kidnapped.*

The leather seat is cold against my cheek, and I can smell something that definitely doesn't belong to me—cologne. Expensive cologne with notes of cedar and smoke and musk. It's not unpleasant, exactly, but it's foreign. *Unknown.* The scent of a stranger.

My chest tightens, and I force myself to remain still. I don't want them to know I'm awake yet.

Someone took me. Someone actually took me and tied me up like I'm some kind of animal. This can't be real. Things like this don't happen to people like me. I work in accounting, for fuck's sake. I spend my play money on books and pay *most* of my bills on time... And I rarely stay up past midnight on weeknights. I don't have enemies. I don't owe money to dangerous people. I don't live a life that should get me bound in the back seat of a stranger's car.

Why me? Why the fuck is this happening to *me* of all people?

The questions keep coming, providing no answers, only more fear.

My head is pounding from whatever was used to knock me out or from the stress I'm feeling right now; I can't tell. It's probably both. My mouth feels cotton-dry, and there's a metallic taste on my tongue that might be blood. My body aches like I've been in this position for hours, muscles stiff and protesting every small movement.

Stay calm. You have to stay calm and think your way out of this.

But it's almost impossible to stay calm when every instinct I have is screaming at me to fight, to *run*, to do anything except lie here helplessly while being driven to who knows where for who knows what purpose.

I try to slow my breathing, counting in and out the way I learned in a yoga class I took last summer. *In for four, hold for four, out for four.* But it comes in sharp, shallow gasps that make my chest burn and my vision blur around the edges. I'm being too loud, which makes me panic even more.

I need to focus on what I *can* control right now.

The rope around my wrists is thick and rough—probably the kind serial killers use in movies. Whoever did this knows what they're doing. The knots are tight, too.

The vehicle drives like it's expensive. And the leather seats probably cost more than I make in a month. This isn't some beat-up van or stolen car. This is someone with money, someone with resources.

The mafia?

Could it be? Fuck.

I strain my ears, trying to catch any sound that might give me a clue about where we're going. No radio. No voices. No GPS giving directions. Just the steady hum of the engine and the occasional crack of a rock being kicked up beneath the car. The silence from the large male in the driver's seat is the most terrifying part of it all.

Who are you? I want to scream. *What do you want from me? Why are you doing this?*

But I keep my mouth shut, because my gut is telling me that staying quiet is safer right now. Let him think I'm still unconscious. Maybe I can learn something that will help me escape. Maybe I can come up with a plan before he realizes I'm awake.

Escape.

How the fuck am I supposed to escape when I'm tied up in the back of a moving car?

I test the bonds around my wrists again, but the rope is unforgiving, with no give in the knots. They've done this before—there's no slack, no loose ends to work with, no hope of slipping free.

How many women has he done this to before me?

I try to push the thought away, but it lingers like a poison in my mind, festering and spreading with each passing second. Am I just the latest in a series? Is there some pattern I fit, some type he prefers?

The car takes a turn, and I slide across the seat, my shoulder bumping against the door with a thud. I look down as I wince and try to hold back a gasp, and I'm suddenly aware of what I'm wearing—my sexy vampire costume from the office Halloween party.

That's right. I'm the office slut.

The memory comes rushing back. I went all out this year, wearing a fitted black corset with intricate lace details, a short black skirt, thigh-high boots, and dramatic vampire makeup complete with fake blood effects and plastic fangs. I'd spent an hour perfecting the blood splatter pattern on my throat and décolletage, wanting to look authentically undead.

If it's still Friday night, I won't be missed until Monday morning when I don't show up for work.

Three days.

No one will even know I'm gone for three fucking days.

My throat closes up so tightly I can barely breathe. Three days is an eternity. Three days is enough time for... for whatever sick plans this psychopath has in mind.

Don't think about it. Don't let your imagination run wild.

But it's too late. My mind is already spinning through possibilities, each one worse than the last. Images from every crime drama I've ever watched, every true crime podcast I've ever listened to, every news story about women who disappeared and were found days or weeks later...

Stop it. Stop it right now. You're going to live through this.

Think about solutions, not problems.

Maybe I can reason with him. Maybe I can make him see that this isn't worth the risk.

Maybe I can convince him to let me go. I could try to pay him. Friday was payday. I should have an entire paycheck in my bank account, minus the $7 I spent on coffee before work and the $26 I spent on a salad and mozzarella sticks for lunch.

I know how naive it sounds. Someone who's willing to kidnap a woman isn't going to be swayed by one measly little paycheck, especially when they drive a car *this* nice.

But what else do I have? Brute force is impossible and escape is currently out of the question.

My mind. My body. They're all I have left.

Can I fuck my way out of this?

Or can I outsmart him?

The car slows slightly, and I feel us turn off one dirty road and onto another, rougher road. Gravel pings against the undercarriage while the driver maneuvers large dips. The ride becomes bumpier, more jarring, and I have to fight to keep my position on the seat.

He's taking me to the middle of fucking nowhere. It's nearly pitch black outside, and I can't see shit through the tinted windows.

He's taking me somewhere no one will hear me scream.

Once again, every true crime story I've ever heard flashes through my mind—they always take them somewhere isolated. Away from help, away from witnesses, away from any hope of rescue.

This is really happening.

This is actually happening to *me*.

I feel the car slow even more, the gravel giving way to the tires. We're climbing now, I think, based on the way my abs flex to keep my body from rolling backward. Up into hills or mountains, away from civilization, away from *safety*.

How far is he taking me? How long have we been driving?

Without any reference points, it's impossible to tell. I could be five miles from my house or fifty. I could be in the same state or halfway across the country by now.

Focus on what you can control.

When he stops the car, when he comes for me, I need to be ready.

Ready for what? Ready to fight? Ready to run? Ready to negotiate my way out of this?

No, I realize.

Ready to *survive*.

The car takes another turn, this one sharper, and I can hear tree branches scraping against the sides of the vehicle. We're in a forest now, deep enough that branches touch the car as we drive past them. The sound is ominous, like skeletal fingers trying to claw their way inside.

Perfect. A forest. Because that's exactly where every horror movie villain takes their victims.

Despite my terror, or maybe because of it, I find myself trying to memorize every detail I can gather. The softer engine sound tells me we're going slower now, maybe ten or fifteen miles per hour. The terrain is rough and getting worse—this isn't a maintained road.

The car slows further, and I can hear something new—music? No, not music. It's distant, muffled by the car windows, but it's definitely not natural.

I think we're almost there.

Wherever 'there' is.

My heart starts hammering even faster, if that's even possible. This is it.

The sounds are getting clearer now—Halloween recordings.

Wolves howling, psychotic laughter, ghosts booing, and beneath it all, a low tune that sounds like it's straight out of a slasher movie.

The car makes one final turn, and I can feel the difference even with my eyes closed—the sense of space around us, the way sound carries differently in a clearing.

We're here.

What kind of psychopath has background music playing at their murder site?

Don't call it that. You don't know that's what this is.

But you know, don't you? Deep down, you know this isn't going to end with him letting you go.

The car finally, mercifully, comes to a stop. The engine cuts off, and sudden silence rushes in like a wave, broken only by the tick of cooling metal and my own ragged breathing.

This is it.

Whatever happens next, this is where it starts, but it doesn't have to be where it ends.

I squeeze my eyes shut and try to make my body go limp, feigning unconsciousness. Maybe if he thinks I'm still out, I'll have some kind of advantage when he comes for me.

Maybe I'll find a way out of this alive.

I hear the driver's door open with a soft click that sounds impossibly loud in the still air. Heavy boots hit the ground.

He's walking around the car. He's taking his time.

Probably savoring the fucking moment.

The footsteps circle the vehicle slowly, like a predator stalking wounded prey. I can feel him looking at me through the windows, studying me, planning his next move. This is a game to him.

Please. Please let me wake up from this nightmare.

But the harsh bite of rope around my wrists is too real, too raw. The leather smell of the car, the dry feeling of fear in my mouth, the sound of those boots—all of it is undeniably, terrifyingly real.

The footsteps stop just outside my door.

He's right there.

One thin piece of glass and metal between me and him.

What's he waiting for?

Finally, the handle above my head clicks, and cool night air rushes in, carrying with it a mixture of scents that make my stomach churn. Earth and decay, smoke and autumn leaves. And something else, something sweet...

Pumpkin?

"It's time to wake up, my night monster."

His voice is deep, rough around the edges, tainted with hardly leashed control and dark amusement. I don't recognize it. It's definitely not anyone I know.

I keep my eyes closed and try to keep my breathing steady, but I'm trembling now. I can't help it.

"I know you're awake, beautiful."

The endearment should feel menacing, but it doesn't. It sounds almost... familiar. Like he knows me.

But that's impossible.

I've never heard this voice before in my life. I would remember it.

"Your pulse is racing," he continues, and I feel the warm press of skin against my throat—rough fingers checking my heartbeat. "And you've been awake for the last ten minutes. Did you really think I couldn't tell?"

How the fuck would he know that?

The hand moves away, but I can still feel the phantom pressure where he touched me. His touch didn't feel violent or threatening, but possessive. Like he was checking on something that belonged to him.

"There's no point in pretending anymore," he says, and I can hear the wicked smile in his words. "We have work to do, you and I."

Work.

What kind of work requires kidnapping someone and driving them into the middle of a fucking forest?

Nothing good, and definitely nothing I want any part of.

But I don't have a choice, do I? Whatever game he's playing, I'm already a piece on his board. The only question now is whether I'm going to be a passive pawn or find a way to become a player and win the game.

Be smart. Assess the situation. Look for opportunities.

Survive.

I open my eyes.

The first thing I see is his massive silhouette looming over me, backlit by moonlight and orange artificial light coming from somewhere behind him. He's tall, much taller than me, with broad shoulders that block my view. I can't see his face clearly with the light shining behind him, but I can feel the intensity of his gaze like heat against my skin.

He's been waiting for this moment.

Anticipating it.

This is all part of his plan. To make me feel small. Helpless. Like I've got nowhere to run.

"Good girl," he says, and something in his voice makes my stomach flip. "Let's get you out of there."

Good girl.

Why do those two little words send a wave of heat through me?

What is wrong with me?

He reaches into the car, and every instinct I have screams at me to fight, to kick, to do something. But with my hands and feet bound, there's nothing I can do except let him lift me from the car like I weigh nothing at all.

Fuck, he's strong.

So much stronger than me.

Fighting him would be useless. He'd pin me down and break me like a toothpick in seconds.

His arms are solid muscle beneath his black button up shirt, and he handles me with a care that feels too gentle for the situation he's put us in. Like he doesn't want to hurt me.

But that doesn't make sense.

None of this makes sense.

As he carries me away from the car, I finally catch my first real glimpse of where we are, and breath hitches in the back of my throat.

Oh my God.

We're in a forest clearing, surrounded by tall trees that stretch up into the star-studded sky. But it's what's in the clearing that makes me forget how to breathe, that makes me question my eyes.

This isn't possible.

What did he knock me out with? I have to be hallucinating. This can't be real.

Dozens upon dozens of jack-o'-lanterns are scattered across the ground like fallen stars, their glowing faces casting flickering shadows in a thick mist that curls around their bases. The fog is so dense I can only see a few feet in any direction, but what I can see looks like something ripped straight from a fever dream or a fairy tale gone wrong.

It's beautiful, yet so terrifying.

It's impossible.

The jack-o'-lanterns are works of art—elaborate, intricate designs that must have taken forever to complete. Some are traditional Halloween faces, triangular eyes and jagged grins that leer at me through the mist. Others are far more complex, with patterns so detailed they can't be real.

How?

How is any of this possible?

What kind of psychopath creates something this elaborate, this beautiful, this absolutely fucking insane? And the Halloween music playing in the background... It polishes the spooky aesthetic.

The magnitude of it is overwhelming. This isn't some makeshift setup thrown together for one night. This is months of planning, professional-level work, more money than most people see in a lifetime.

He did all of this.

For *me*.

But I can't understand why.

"Welcome to your nightmare, night monster," he murmurs against my ear, his breath warm against the fake blood on my neck. "I hope you're ready to play."

Play.

He called this playing.

What kind of game requires an elaborate field of jack-o'-lanterns in the middle of a forest?

What kind of game starts with kidnapping?

As he carries me deeper into the impossible wonderland he's created, as the fog swirls around us like it's alive and the jack-o'-lanterns are watching us with their carved eyes,

I realize that everything I thought I knew about my life has just been shattered.

This is really happening.

This is actually happening to me.

And I have no idea how it's going to end.

CHAPTER 2
THE HUNT BEGINS

Luke

She has no idea how long I've been planning this night, and watching her small, helpless form curled on my back seat fills me with a satisfaction so deep it's almost wrong. Like I'm a god who's finally claimed his most perfect creation.

I glance in the rearview mirror as I navigate the final winding curves of the forest road, drinking in every exquisite detail of the woman who belongs to me. Even bound and unconscious, she's breathtaking in that vampire costume she chose so carefully—*for me*, whether she consciously knew it or not. The fake blood from her makeup has smeared across her pale throat during the drive, and her dark auburn hair with that striking white streak fans across the leather like spilled wine. She looks stunning, too pure for this world, and tonight I'm going to corrupt her so thoroughly she'll never want to leave me.

My night monster. My obsession. My beautiful, brilliant addiction that I've spent endless time and money to possess.

I grin beneath my devil mask as I check my watch—10:47 PM. Perfect timing, just as I planned. The fog machines activated automatically twenty minutes ago based on the GPS trigger I installed, and by now the entire patch should be shrouded in that ethereal mist that will make everything feel like she's stepping into another world entirely.

Her world. The world I built specifically for her.

My hands tighten on the steering wheel as anticipation courses through me like a drug I've been mainlining for fifteen months. Fifteen months of planning, of obsessing over every little detail, and it all comes down to the next few hours. I've thought through every possible scenario so many times I could execute this plan in my sleep. I've run contingencies for weather, for equipment failure, for almost anything. I have backup plans for my backup plans, because failure is not an option when it comes to her.

Never when it comes to her.

But there's still that familiar nervous energy thrumming beneath my skin—the same feeling I used to get before hostile takeovers, except this is infinitely more important than any business deal I've ever orchestrated. This is about claiming what's mine and proving that some men don't just love.

They possess.

They consume.

And they can mold the world in service of their obsession.

This is about her, and us, and showing her that I will literally tear down mountains and rebuild forests to own every piece of her soul.

The memory of the conversation that sparked all of this is burned into my mind, replaying in perfect detail every single day for fifteen months. We'd been curled together in bed after I'd fucked her so thoroughly she could barely speak, her body still trembling against my chest while rain drummed against the windows. She'd just finished reading some erotic horror novel—Carving for Cara—and when she was telling me about it—fuck—I couldn't help but notice how breathless and needy she was, desperately trying to hide the darkness that book awakened in her.

But I saw it.

Does she even remember?

"Can you imagine?" she had whispered, her fingers tracing patterns on my skin like she was writing her deepest secrets directly onto my body. "Being hunted like that? Chased through a corn field and then fucked in a pumpkin patch?"

"Caught and claimed in the middle of all those pumpkins, with the fog swirling around you and no escape, no choice but to surrender completely to someone who'll never let you go?"

My cock twitches at the memory.

I remember the exact moment her breathing changed, the way she shifted against me like the very thought was making her wet. The way she kept coming back to certain details over and over again—the Halloween setting, the genuine terror mixed with arousal, the way the female main character ultimately chose her captor over freedom.

Or was it that she *found* freedom from within *him*?

Either way, my girl didn't just want the fantasy. She *needed* it. Craved it like an addict craves their next fix.

And I've spent fifteen months becoming the perfect dealer.

"The girl in the book fought at first," Seraphina had continued, her voice getting softer, almost confessional. "She was terrified and confused and had no idea who he was or why he'd chosen her. But by the end... by the end she didn't want to escape anymore. She *wanted* to be caught. She wanted to be claimed and to belong to someone who would burn the world for her."

That conversation planted the seed. And that seed grew into so many glorious things.

Does she even remember it?

I made it happen. Because that's what I do best—I fixate. And I don't stop until I've satisfied that untamed hunger.

Because that's what this is. Total consumption. Complete possession. The willingness to burn down the world and rebuild it in a way that meets all of her desires.

The first call I made was to Jensen Landscaping, and I told them I needed to purchase and clear a specific section of forest about an hour outside the city. I didn't sleep for three weeks while the land acquisition was being negotiated—I'd lie awake staring at satellite photos, measuring distances, calculating sight lines, mapping every tree that would need to be removed. The cost was more than most people's houses, but money means nothing when you're building an empire for the woman who owns your soul.

I know it will be worth every fucking penny.

The clearing and initial earth preparation took another two months of me driving out to the site multiple times a week, watching the crews work, ensuring every detail met my exact specifications. I hired four different teams to prevent any single group from understanding the full scope of my obsession. One team handled the tree removal and ground leveling—I stood there for hours, directing them which trees to spare and which to destroy based on how I imagined chasing her. Another installed the underground infrastructure—power lines, water access, and the network of pipes that would eventually feed the fog machine system. The third crew planted the pumpkin patch earlier in the year and tended to it throughout the summer and early fall. The fourth and final crew carved over a hundred pumpkins this week, equipping each one with a yellow-light candle on a timer to go off all night long.

This wasn't a matter of scattering some seeds and hoping for the best—I wanted variety, different sizes and colors and growth patterns that would create the perfect spooky setting for tonight.

Each one is a prop in the elaborate theater I've created to break her down and remake her.

Some are enormous—nearly two hundred pounds that she'll have to navigate around, creating natural obstacles. Others are small enough to trip over, perfectly placed to send her stumbling when she's running in pure terror. The variety creates chaos and confusion in the field, forcing her into panic decisions while I maintain complete control over every option available to her.

Every pathway leads exactly where I want it to go.

Every dead end was strategically placed to drive her deeper into my web.

Every route to freedom will be eliminated until surrender becomes her only choice.

The invoice for the carvers alone was more than Seraphina's annual salary, but I would have paid ten times that amount to ensure every detail was perfect. I *need* tonight to be perfect. For us.

But the most expensive part wasn't the labor or the materials—it was the technology. The fog machine system required consultation with three different special effects companies before we found one willing to tackle the scale I had in mind. We're not talking about a simple dry ice setup or a basic party fog machine. This is a professional-grade atmospheric system with programmable density controls, scent injection capabilities, and GPS-triggered activation.

Because I wanted the fog to be rolling when we arrived. I wanted the atmosphere to be perfect from the first moment she sees what I've built.

Every detail serves a larger plan.

Every element is designed to give her the ultimate high.

The sound system was another challenge entirely. How does one create ambient audio for a pumpkin patch without making it obvious where the speakers are hidden? How does one ensure consistent volume and quality throughout such a large space?

Six months of acoustic testing and equipment trials.

Hidden speakers throughout the patch, synchronized to respond to proximity sensors.

When she runs, the sound will follow her. When she stops, it will *surround* her.

It's an immersive experience.

I check the mirror again and see her starting to stir, consciousness returning right on schedule. The timing couldn't be more perfect if I'd planned it down to the minute.

Which, of course, I did.

The sedative was calculated to wear off exactly as we arrived. Dr. Williams was very precise about dosage based on her height and weight.

Everything has been calculated. Everything has been planned.

Except for how she'll actually react when she realizes what I've done for her. How far I've gone for her. For *us*.

That's the one variable I can't control, the one element that makes this entire thing either the most romantic gesture in history or a complete fucking disaster. I know she wants this—she literally described it to me in detail. But this...

Can she handle it?

She can.

She has to.

This is what she wanted.

This is her fantasy come to life.

The forest opens up ahead of us, revealing the cleared space that's been my obsession for over a year. Even knowing every detail of what I've created, the sight of it still takes my breath away. The fog machines have done their work perfectly, creating thick, rolling clouds that transform the patch into something unreal. The jack-o'-lanterns glow through the mist, their carved faces appearing and disappearing as the fog shifts and swirls around them.

It's perfect.

It's absolutely fucking perfect.

Like something from a dream. Or a *nightmare*.

I park the car at the edge of the clearing and cut the engine, savoring this moment before everything changes. Behind me, I can hear Seraphina's breathing shift to the sharp, quick pants of fear and disorientation.

My cock strains inside my pants, pushing to get out.

Fear first. Then confusion. Then gradually, slowly, the realization that this isn't actually about taking something from her.

It's about giving her everything she wants.

I take a moment to check my reflection in the rearview mirror, adjusting the blood-red devil mask that's been hanging there for the past hour. It covers my eyes and nose but leaves my mouth exposed—perfect for tasting her when I catch her. I want her to see exactly how much I'm enjoying this game we're about to play.

The mask was custom-made for this. Hand-crafted leather with metallic accents that will catch the jack-o'-lantern light perfectly.

Because every detail matters if this is going to be perfect.

For tonight, I'm truly a stranger to her. She won't know who I am or why I've brought her here. Not until the end.

The grand finale.

I can feel my heart rate picking up as I prepare to get out of the car, adrenaline flooding my system. This is it. There's no going back now.

She's going to love this.

She *has* to love this.

Because I've put everything I am into making this night perfect for her.

And if she doesn't... *fuck*, I don't know what I'll do.

I climb out of the car slowly, savoring the sound of my boots on gravel. Each step is a countdown to her awakening, to the moment when she realizes that her darkest fantasy has found her whether she was ready for it or not.

Fear is the ultimate aphrodisiac when you control every variable.

And she is safe. Safer than she's ever been in her life.

Because I would kill anyone who tried to hurt her.

I would burn down cities to keep her from harm.

But I'll also ensure she never escapes from what we're about to become.

I just have to break her a little... to help her understand.

The night air is cold but not painful, carrying the scent of woodsmoke from the fire pit I had installed at the center of the patch. The fog machines are working perfectly. Even the moon is cooperating—full and bright above the trees like a spotlight on our stage.

It's coming together exactly as I envisioned.

I circle the car slowly, taking my time, letting her wonder what I'm doing out here in the darkness. Through the windows, I can see her trying to feign unconsciousness, but her pulse is hammering visibly at her throat. Even in the dim light, I can see the rapid flutter of her heartbeat, and it makes something possessive and primal rise in my chest.

She's mine.

She's always been mine, from the moment I first saw her.

Tonight I'm just going to make it official.

I check my watch one more time—10:52 PM. The night is young, and I have so much planned for her. The grand finale will elevate everything that came before. But first, she needs to experience the fantasy fully. She needs to run and be caught and pleasured and claimed by a stranger who wants her more than anything else in this world.

She needs to surrender completely.

My hand finds the small remote in my pocket—the one that controls the lighting at the patch center, the one that will transform our hunting ground when the moment is right.

When I reach her door, I pause with my hand on the handle. This is the last moment before everything changes. The last second of anticipation. After this, there's no going back.

I hope you're ready, baby.

I hope you're ready to discover what you're really capable of and how far you'll fall into darkness.

I hope you're ready to be hunted by someone who's already decided you'll never get away.

I open the door and let the cool night air rush in, carrying with it the scent of my stage. The combination creates an atmosphere that's both familiar and otherworldly, natural and supernatural.

"It's time to wake up, my night monster."

The nickname feels perfect on my tongue—she looks like a vampire princess in that skimpy little costume, all pale skin and dark lashes and blood-red lips. But tonight, *I'm* the predator. I'm the one who hunts.

I can see her trying to control her breathing, trying to maintain the illusion of unconsciousness, but her body betrays her completely. The rapid pulse, the tension in her shoulders, the way her fingers curl slightly even though she's trying to stay limp.

She's terrified.

And it makes my cock strain harder. *Fuck.* I need her.

"I know you're awake, beautiful. Your pulse is racing."

I reach out and press my fingers to her throat, feeling the frantic flutter of her heartbeat against my fingertips. I can feel how warm she is, how *alive* she is. The sensation sends heat straight to my fucking cock.

This is about fulfilling my darkest fantasies too.

"There's no point in pretending anymore. We have work to do, you and I."

She opens her eyes, and even in the darkness, I can see the mix of terror and confusion and something else—something that makes my blood sing with anticipation. She's afraid, yes, but there's a part of her that's already responding to this. Already awakening to possibilities she's never allowed herself to fully acknowledge, let alone explore.

There she is.

My beautiful, brilliant, completely irreplaceable night monster.

And she's ready to play our game.

"Good girl," I murmur, and I don't miss the way her breath catches at the praise. "Let's get you out of there."

I lift her from the car with deliberate care, cradling her against my chest like she's made of glass. She's so perfectly sized to fit against me, so exactly right in my arms that it's like holding a missing piece of myself.

I wanted her to feel cherished even while she's been kidnapped.

As I carry her toward the pumpkin patch, I watch her face in the moonlight, memorizing every expression as she takes in the scene I've created for her. Her eyes go wide as she processes the magnitude of it.

This is her fantasy.

Her deepest desire.

Her most secret longings brought to life in a world we can actually inhabit.

"Welcome to your nightmare," I whisper against her ear. "I hope you're ready to play."

Because I've been ready for months.

I've been dreaming of this night since the moment you told me what you wanted.

I've been planning and building and creating, and now finally, *finally* it's time to show her how far I'm willing to go.

It's time to hunt her through the world I built just for her.

To catch her and claim her and keep her forever.

Starting *now*.

CHAPTER 3
WELCOME TO THE NIGHTMARE

Seraphina

I stumble as he sets me on my feet, my legs weak from being bound for so long. He doesn't try to steady me, just watches with that unnerving stillness as I find my balance before pulling a knife from his back pocket and cutting me free of my binds in practiced, easy movements. In the moonlight, I can see him more clearly now—tall and broad-shouldered, wearing an unbuttoned black shirt that shows glimpses of tattoos across his chest. His pants are expensive-looking slacks, and even his belt looks like it cost more than my rent.

But it's the mask that makes my entire body go still. It's like something out of a nightmare, distorted angles and demonic features that seem to leer at me in the flickering pumpkin light.

He's the devil. He's actually dressed like the fucking devil.

"Beautiful, isn't it?" His voice carries a note of pride, like he's showing off a work of art. "I had it designed just for you."

Just for me? The words make my head spin. How could he possibly know me well enough to—

"I don't understand," I whisper, my voice hardly audible over the sound of my own heartbeat pounding in my ears. "What do you want from me? Why are you doing this?"

He steps closer, and I instinctively back away, my boots sinking into the soft earth.

"I told you. I want to play a game." His voice drops to a deadly whisper that makes my stomach tighten despite my terror. "A very simple game."

The fog swirls around us, so thick I can't see beyond the immediate glow of the nearest jack-o'-lanterns. The rest of the maze disappears into that spooky mist.

"What kind of game?" I ask, though I'm not sure I want to know the answer.

He's handsome in a way that would make angels weep—sharp cheekbones and bright green eyes, medium brown hair styled perfectly even with the mask, and a short, clean-cut beard that frames a wicked grin. Everything about him screams *danger*.

I feel like I should recognize this face. Like I should know who he is. But my mind is blank, terror short-circuiting my ability to think clearly. All I know is that he's the most beautiful monster I've ever seen.

Play the part, some distant part of my mind whispers. *He wants you terrified. He wants you confused. Give him what he wants until you can figure out how to escape.*

"I don't know you," I say when he doesn't respond, my voice shaking. "I don't understand why you've done this to me."

His smile is slow and predatory, showing perfect white teeth. "You will. Before this night is over, you'll understand everything." He steps closer, close enough that I can smell that expensive cologne again. "But first, we're going to play."

"What kind of—"

"I'm going to give you exactly what you've always wanted," he says, cutting me off. His voice is rough with desire. "I'm going to hunt you through this pumpkin patch. I'm going to chase you until your heart is pounding and your legs are giving out beneath you and you're running on nothing but pure adrenaline and will to survive."

My mouth goes dry. This is insane. This is absolutely fucking insane.

"And when I catch you—not if, but *when*—I'm going to have my fun with you." His green eyes are burning with an intensity that makes my knees weak. "I'm going to touch you and taste you and fuck you in ways that will make you forget your own name."

Oh my god.

"But here's the thing that makes it interesting," he continues, circling me lazily like a predator sizing up his prey. "You're going to run. You're going to run like your life depends on it, because in a way, it *does*. The woman you are right now? She ends tonight. What you become after I'm done with you? That's entirely up to how well you play the game."

I can't breathe. The combination of terror and confusion is making my head spin. "And if I don't run?" I challenge him.

His laugh is dark and throaty and absolutely terrifying. "Oh, you'll run. Every instinct you have is going to scream at you to run." He leans in close, his warm breath sending chills down my spine. "The question is how long you can keep it up before your body betrays you and you start wanting to be caught."

This can't be happening.

But even as I think about it, I can feel it awakening deep in my chest. The part of me that responds to the promise in his voice, to the careful way he's watching me through the mask. That part of me that whispers *what if* instead of *help me.*

No. Absolutely fucking not. I am not going to Stockholm syndrome myself with my own kidnapper.

"I'll scream," I threaten, though my voice lacks any real conviction. "Someone will hear me."

"Go ahead," he says with that same terrifying smile. "Scream all you want. We're five miles from the nearest paved road and ten miles from the nearest house. The only things that will hear you are the wolves." He pauses, head tilted like he's listening. "Actually, I think I hear them already."

As if summoned by his words, a low howl echoes through the trees, followed by another. The sound makes the hair on the back of my neck stand up.

"Now," he says, stepping back and giving me space. "I'm going to count to ten. When I reach ten, I'm coming after you. You'd better hope you can run fast in those boots, night monster."

This is really happening.

"One."

Fuck!

My heart lurches into my throat. He's serious. He's actually serious.

"Two."

I look around wildly, trying to orient myself in the field of pumpkins. The fog makes it impossible to see beyond what's directly in front of me, and the pathways wind between the pumpkins in patterns I can't follow. But there —beyond the jack-o'-lanterns, I can make out the dark shapes of trees. If I can reach the tree line, maybe I can lose him in the forest.

"Three."

Run. Just run.

"Four."

My feet are already moving before my brain catches up, carrying me deeper into the pumpkin patch. The soft earth is treacherous under my boots, and I stumble over a pumpkin vine almost immediately, barely catching myself before I fall face-first into a particularly menacing jack-o'-lantern.

"Five."

His voice is already getting fainter as I put distance between us, but it carries clearly through the fog. There's amusement in it, like he's enjoying watching me panic.

Focus. You need to focus.

I force myself to slow down slightly, picking my way more carefully between the pumpkins. The field is more complex than I initially realized—every time I think I've found a straight path to the trees, it curves back on itself or dead-ends in a cluster of particularly elaborate and creepy carvings.

"Six."

The fog is getting thicker the deeper I go, swirling around my legs like ghostly fingers. The sweet pumpkin smell is stronger here too, making everything feel that much more dreamlike and surreal. My corset is making it hard to get a deep breath, and I can already feel sweat gathering at the base of my neck despite the cool air.

"Seven."

I risk a glance back and can't see him anymore. The fog has swallowed him completely, leaving only the glow of jack-o'-lanterns to mark where I've been. But I can feel him back there, waiting. Watching. Counting.

"Eight."

There. I spot what looks like a clear path toward the trees and start running full speed, my boots pounding against the dirt. The sound seems impossibly loud in the stillness, but I can't help it. Terror is driving me now, pure survival instinct that demands speed over stealth.

"Nine."

Almost there. I can see the edge of the patch now, the dark bulk of the forest beyond. If I can just reach the trees, I can lose him in the undergrowth. I can find my way back to a road, to civilization, to help. To anywhere but here.

Please. Please let me make it.

"Ten."

The word echoes through the fog behind me like a goddamn death sentence, and suddenly the night explodes with sound. Heavy footsteps pounding against the earth, moving fast and getting faster. He's not just following me —he's hunting me with an intensity so overwhelming I nearly collapse on the spot.

Oh God. Oh God, he's actually doing it.

I reach the edge of the patch and plunge into the forest without looking back, branches catching at my costume and hair. The moonlight barely penetrates the canopy here, turning everything into a maze of shadows and uncertain footing. But I don't care. I just run.

Behind me, I can hear him crashing through the trees. He's fast—much faster than I expected—and he's gaining ground quickly. *Too* quickly.

How can he be this fast?

My lungs are burning, my legs already shaking, but I force myself to keep going. I have to keep going. I'm not ready for him to catch me.

A root catches my ankle and I go down hard, skinning my palms on the rough bark of a fallen log. For a moment, I just lie there gasping, my whole body trembling with exhaustion and terror.

The footsteps behind me have stopped.

Where is he?

I hold my breath, straining to hear over the sound of my own heartbeat pounding in my ears. The forest has gone completely silent, like even the wolves are holding their breath to see what happens next.

Maybe I lost him. Maybe he—

A twig snaps somewhere to my left, and my blood turns cold. He's not behind me anymore. He's circling me like a wolf stalking wounded prey.

I have to move. I have to get up and move right fucking now.

I struggle to my feet and immediately realize my mistake. In my panic, I've lost all sense of direction. The trees all look the same in the moonlight, and I can't tell which way leads back to the pumpkin patch and which way leads deeper into the forest.

Another sound—this time to my right. Closer.

He's playing with me.

This isn't just about catching me, I realize. He's enjoying this. He's drawing it out, letting me think I might escape just so he can take that hope away piece by piece.

"Marco," his voice calls through the trees, dripping with dark humor.

I don't answer, don't move, don't dare to even breathe.

"Polo," he says anyway, and his voice is definitely closer now.

Run.

I take off again, crashing through the forest with no regard for stealth or direction. I just need to get away from that voice, from the terrible certainty that he's going to catch me no matter what I do.

But even as I run, some traitorous part of my mind is whispering that this is exactly what I've always fantasized about. Being chased. Being hunted.

And a masked man, of all fucking things.

Stop it, I tell myself fiercely. *He kidnapped you. He's a psychopath who kidnapped you and tied you up in his car. This is not a fantasy. This is not something you want.*

But my body seems to have other ideas. Despite the terror, the exhaustion, and everything logical and sane screaming at me to get away, I can feel heat building low in my stomach, trickling down between my thighs. My skin feels hypersensitive, every brush of cool air making me shiver.

What is wrong with me?

"Getting tired yet, night monster?" His voice is practically on top of me now, and I realize with dawning horror that I ran in the wrong direction. The pumpkin patch is visible through the trees ahead—I'm right back where I started.

I spin around, trying to locate him, but the fog has followed me into the forest and everything is a blur.

"I can hear your heart racing," he says, and his voice seems to come from everywhere at once. "I can practically smell your fear. It's intoxicating."

Where is he?

"But there's something else, isn't there?" His voice drops to a whisper that carries perfectly through the still air. "Something you don't want to admit to yourself."

No.

"Your body knows what it wants, even if your mind hasn't caught up yet."

Strong hands grab my waist from behind, and I scream into the night.

CHAPTER 4

CAUGHT

Seraphina

"Got you," he growls against my ear, his breath hot. His arms are like steel bands around me, holding me effortlessly despite my struggles.

No, no, no. Fuck!

I twist in his grip, trying to break free, but he's so much stronger than me it's almost laughable. My feet barely touch the ground as he lifts me against his chest, and I can feel the hard planes of his body through his open shirt. The tattoos I glimpsed earlier are more visible now—intricate smoke and tree designs that disappear beneath the fabric.

Why me? All I wanted was to go to the office party in this slutty little costume and take someone home with me at the end of the night. Instead, I'm in the middle of fucking nowhere with a masked man at least twice my size, and I didn't even get fucked.

"Shh," he says, practically dragging me back toward the pumpkin patch like I weigh nothing at all. I fight against him, but it's no use. "You ran well, night monster. Better than I expected. But you weren't fast enough."

The fog parts around us as we emerge from the forest, revealing the glowing jack-o'-lanterns scattered throughout the clearing. Up close, they're even more elaborate than I initially realized—some are true works of art, with intricate patterns carved into their surfaces that throw complex shadows across the ground. Others are genuinely terrifying, all sharp angles and menacing expressions.

This is insane. All of this is absolutely insane.

He carries me to what I think is the center of the field, where several pathways converge around a particularly large pumpkin. This one isn't carved—instead, it sits whole and perfectly untouched, surrounded by thick vines that sprawl across the ground in tangled patterns.

"Perfect," he says, throwing me down beside the pumpkin. "Absolutely perfect."

Before I can even think about running again, he's grabbing my wrists and stretching them over my head, securing them in a way that spreads me wide. But instead of rope this time, he's using the pumpkin vines themselves, twisting them around my arms and tightening intricate knots. I kick at him as he moves to my feet, pulling my legs apart until they won't stretch any more. I feel exposed to not only him, but the entire field around us. It's like each carved pumpkin is watching, grinning as they wait to see what happens next.

Who ties someone up with *pumpkin vines* of all things?

"They're stronger than you'd think," he says like he's reading my mind. "Flexible, but they don't break easily." He leans closer, his voice dropping to that dangerous, spine-tingling whisper again. "I thought you'd appreciate the festivity of it."

The vines are rough against my skin, and their sharp little thorns bite into my wrists as I pull against them, but he's right. They're too strong.

"There," he says, stepping back to admire his work. "I've got you right where I want you, and now you can't run from what you really want."

What I really want?

"You don't know anything about what I want," I snap at him.

But the truth is, the terror is still there, loud and in my face, but it's mixing with something else now... That something makes my skin feel hypersensitive and my pulse race.

"Your mouth says one thing," he murmurs, kneeling over me. "But your body is telling a very different story."

He's right, and I hate him for it. My body is responding to him and this entire fucked-up situation in ways that make no sense. My breathing is shallow and quick, my skin feels flushed and hot, and there's a growing ache between my thighs.

What is wrong with me?

"Look at you," he growls, reaching out to trace one finger along my collarbone. His touch burns like fire against my bare skin. "Your pupils are dilated. Your pulse is racing. Your skin is flushed." His finger trails lower, following the lace edge of my corset. "And I bet if I checked, I'd find you're wet for me already."

Oh god.

"You're wrong," I whisper, but it comes out breathless and unconvincing.

"Let's find out, shall we?" There's an amused twinkle in his eyes as he watches me through the mask. Like he already knows what he'll find.

His hands are on my thighs before I can process what he's doing, sliding up beneath my short skirt at a tortuously slow speed.

I should fight him. I should scream.

Someone might hear me.

I should do anything except lay here trembling while a stranger—a *kidnapper*—touches me like he fucking owns me.

But that's exactly what I do. I lay here, bound by pumpkin vines and my own traitorous desires, while he begins exploring my body.

"*Fuck*," he hisses when his fingers find the lace of my underwear. "You're soaked."

Shame. Hot, burning shame floods through me, followed immediately by arousal so intense it makes my knees quake. How can I be turned on by this? How can my body betray me so completely?

"Please," I whisper, though I'm not sure if I'm begging him to stop or to continue.

"Please what, night monster?" His fingers trace the outer edge of my panties, not quite touching where I need him most. "Please stop? Please don't?" His voice drops again, throaty and entangled with desire. "Or please don't stop?"

I can't answer. I literally cannot form words while his hands are on me like this, while he's looking at me like I'm his next meal.

"That's what I thought," he says, confirming what I'm too ashamed to say out loud.

He pulls my panties aside and slides one finger inside me, slow and deliberate and undeniably devastating. I arch against the restraints, a sound escaping my throat that's part moan, part sob.

This is wrong. This is so wrong.

But it feels too good to be wrong.

"You're so fucking tight," he groans, adding a second finger and making me cry out. "So perfect. Your pussy was waiting for me, wasn't it? Look at it," he says as he removes his fingers and shows me how wet they are. "You're weeping for me, baby."

His thumb finds my clit at the same time his fingers plunge back inside me, curling at that perfect angle, and suddenly I can't think at all. There's only sensation—heat and pressure and pleasure so intense it walks the line of pain.

"That's it," he says, his voice low and throaty. "Let go. Stop fighting what you want."

I can't want this. I *shouldn't* want this.

But my body is singing under his touch, every nerve ending alive and desperate for more. The vines around my wrists keep me from folding in on myself as he works me with large fingers, bringing me closer and closer to the edge of sanity.

"You're close, aren't you?" He leans in, his lips pressing against my clit as he continues pumping into me. "I can feel your pussy gripping my fingers like a fucking vice. How desperate you are. How much you want this." Each puff of his breath makes me jolt at the overwhelming sensation.

Yes. The word echoes in my head, but I refuse to say it out loud.

"Come for me, night monster," he whispers, and his voice so demanding it sends a new wave of chills through me. "Show me how pretty you are when you come all over my fingers."

His wet tongue flicks against my clit in tandem with the thrust of his fingers, and I shatter.

The orgasm hits me like lightning, tearing through my body with an intensity that makes me scream. My vision goes black, my muscles lock, and for a moment I'm lost to the ecstasy of *him*.

When I finally come back to myself, I'm shaking and gasping and completely horrified by what just happened. He's still touching me, still moving his fingers gently inside me, drawing out aftershocks that make me whimper. I want to close my legs to relieve how sensitive and exposed I'm feeling, but the vines stop me.

"Beautiful," he murmurs, finally withdrawing his hand and bringing it to his mouth. "Absolutely fucking beautiful." He opens his mouth, letting his tongue roll over his fingers in a flat, lazy motion. He tastes me. I mean, *really* tastes me, licking until there's none of me left on his fingers.

I can't look away from him. I can't believe I just... that I actually...

How is this real?

"Mmm," he moans, reaching for something at his belt. "I've had a taste, but I think I need more."

The knife appears in his hand—the same silver blade he used to cut my ropes earlier. The moonlight hits it perfectly, making it gleam brightly against the dark night.

He's going to kill me. He's going to kill me and I just let him—

I inhale sharply, jamming my eyes shut as he brings it to my cheek. He uses the flat of the blade to trace patterns across my cold skin. The metal is icy against my overheated flesh, making me shiver and arch despite my fear.

"Relax," he says, noting my tension. "I won't hurt you. Well," his smile turns sinister, "not in any way you won't thoroughly enjoy."

The knife trails down my throat, following the fake blood from my vampire costume. He pauses at my collarbone, using just the tip to trace the edge of my corset.

This is insane. *He's* insane.

And I'm fucking insane for not hating this.

"Do you know what I'm going to do to you?" he questions, and I can tell one of his eyebrows is arched by the way his forehead crinkles above his mask.

I shake my head silently.

"I'm going to taste every inch of you," he says, sliding the knife lower. "I'm going to use my mouth and my tongue and my teeth until you're begging for more." The blade catches on a loose thread of my costume, cutting through it effortlessly. "And then I'm going to fuck you until you forget your own name."

Fuck.

The crude words should horrify me, but instead they send heat shooting straight between my legs. My body is already responding again, already wanting more of him.

"But first," he says, cutting my panties off and falling to his knees between my legs, "I want to taste what I've done to you."

His hands are on my thighs again, spreading me wider as he presses them into the dirt, and then his mouth is on me and I'm lost once more.

Lost to him. To this place. To the awakened feeling growing inside my chest.

He doesn't tease this time, and doesn't build slowly. His tongue finds my clit immediately and works it in firm circles, making me arch and strain against the vines holding me in place. The feeling is overwhelming—his hot mouth, the rough texture of his beard against my inner thighs, the cool October air hitting the most sensitive parts of me.

I try to hold back, try to maintain some shred of dignity, but it's useless. Within seconds, I'm grinding against his mouth out of desperation, chasing another orgasm that I shouldn't want but need more than air.

"That's it," he growls against me, the vibration of his voice making me cry out. "Don't fight it. Give me what I want."

He slides two fingers back inside me while his mouth continues its assault on my clit, occasionally dipping between my folds, and the sensation is too much. I come again, even harder this time, my whole body convulsing as wave after wave of pleasure crashes over me.

This is wrong. This is so wrong, but it feels so...

When he finally pulls away, I'm hanging limp in my restraints, completely spent. My legs feel like jelly. I let my head fall back, collapsing into the dirt below me.

I watch him through hooded eyes as he rises to his full height, eyes never leaving my body. "Absolutely perfect."

He picks up the knife again, and he cuts through the vines holding me in place. They fall away, and I immediately scramble backwards, my legs too weak to hold me.

He stops me before I collide with the giant pumpkin, and his hands are surprisingly gentle.

"Easy," he says, his eyes shockingly kind. "This is only the beginning. Don't quit on me now."

I stare up at him in confusion, taking in the sharp angles of his face in the moonlight. The devil mask is still there, but it's easy to see how devastatingly handsome he is. His green eyes are bright with satisfaction, and what looks almost like... fondness?

That can't be right.

"I don't understand," I whisper, my voice hoarse from screaming through my orgasms. "What do you want from me?"

His smile is dark and predatory. "I want you to run again."

What?

"Run again?" I stare at him like he's lost his mind. "You just... and now you want me to..."

"Run," he says again, stepping back and giving me space, but his voice goes cold. "The night is young. We're just getting started. Now *run*."

I look around the field, trying to process what just happened. My body is still humming with the aftereffects of two orgasms, my mind reeling with confusion and shame and fear.

He could have done anything to me just now. He could have...

But he didn't. He pleasured me until I cried out for him, then cut me free and told me to run again.

What kind of monster is he?

"Why?" I ask, daring to question him.

"Because the chase is only half the fun," he says, his voice rich with dark promise. "And because I'm not nearly done with you yet."

I look toward the forest, then back toward the pumpkin patch. Every instinct I have is screaming at me to run toward the trees, to try to escape into the darkness and find help. But another part of me is curious about what will happen if I stay. If I play his game.

"Choose quickly," he says, and there's a spark of amusement in his voice now. "I'm going to start counting again in about ten seconds, and this time I won't be quite so... gentle when I catch you."

Gentle? I almost laugh at the absurdity of it. Nothing about what just happened was gentle.

But looking at him now, at the predatory gleam in his eyes and the way he's watching me like a cat watching a mouse, I realize he's probably right.

Run.

I break into a full sprint, willing my legs to hold me upright.

Behind me, I hear his low chuckle echo through the fog.

And then the hunt begins again.

CHAPTER 5
INTO DARKNESS

Seraphina

I run through the patch, my boots silent on the soft earth as I navigate between the glowing jack-o'-lanterns. This section feels different from where we were before—the pumpkins here are larger, their carved faces more menacing than the others. The fog is thicker too, swirling around my legs and making it impossible to see more than a few feet ahead.

There has to be a way out.

But I'm starting to doubt myself. Every path I take seems to curve back on itself, leading me in circles through the field of tangled vines and pumpkins. Every time I think

I've found a route toward the forest, it dead-ends in a cluster of particularly terrifying jack-o'-lanterns or curves back toward the center where he tasted me.

Behind me, I can hear him moving through the field. He's not rushing this time, showing me he's not feeling desperate. Instead, he's stalking me with the confidence of an apex predator.

I change direction, heading toward what I think is the perimeter of the field. The fog is so thick here that the jack-o'-lanterns seem to float in empty space, their glowing faces appearing and disappearing like something out of a nightmare.

Focus. You need to focus and find a way out of here.

But it's hard to focus when my body is still buzzing from his touch. I can still feel his hands on my skin, his tongue on my clit. The memory makes the ache return between my thighs, and I hate myself for it.

What is wrong with me? He kidnapped me.

But I know it's more complicated than that. Because I didn't fight him, not really. And when he made me come —*twice*—I didn't just endure it. I participated. I arched into his touch and moaned and begged for more with my body if not my words.

Stop thinking about it. Just focus on getting out of here.

I round another pumpkin and find myself face-to-face with a dead end—three enormous jack-o'-lanterns arranged in a semicircle, their carved faces grinning at me in the fog. And they're blocking the only path forward.

Damn it.

I turn to backtrack and freeze. He's standing at the mouth of the pathway, silhouetted against the glow of the jack-o'-lanterns behind him. Even in the fog, I can see the victory in his posture, the way he's watching me like I'm exactly where he wanted me to be.

"Such a clever girl," he says, his voice carrying clearly through the still air. A wolf howls in the distance behind him. "But not clever enough to escape me."

I back against the carved pumpkins, their rough leaves and vines catching on my costume. "Please," I whisper. "I don't understand why I'm here."

"I want you to stop hiding from who you are," he says, and there's a hint of frustration in his voice now. "I want you to stop fighting what you clearly want."

"I don't want this," I protest, but my voice shakes with uncertainty. "This is crazy."

"Your mouth keeps saying that," he murmurs, reaching me and pressing one hand against the pumpkin beside my head. "But your body is begging to be touched." He leans in, and I can feel the heat radiating off his body. "To be tasted." His voice dips with his head. "To be *fucked*."

My pulse is racing, and the ache between my thighs gets worse. It's almost painful now. *Fuck*, I'm getting turned on again.

This can't be normal. This isn't how normal people react to being kidnapped.

"Look at you," he says, his free hand tracing the line of my throat. "Everything about your body is screaming for me." His fingers trail lower, drifting over my stomach. "The way you press your thighs together to relieve the ache. The way you hold your head back, exposing your throat to me. They way I know your pussy is already dripping for me again."

Oh god.

"You don't know anything about me," I whisper, holding his heated gaze.

"Mmm," he looks me up and down, biting at his bottom lip. "Let's find out."

This time I don't even pretend to fight when his hands

slide up my thighs, hiking my skirt over my hips and out of the way.

"Fuck," he breathes when his fingers find me. "I knew you'd be soaked."

The word makes me whimper, and I hate that sound almost as much as I hate how right he is. I *am* soaked— wetter than before, if that's even possible. My body is betraying me completely, responding to him with an eagerness that makes no sense.

"Please," I whisper again, and this time I know I'm not asking him to stop.

"Please what, night monster?" His fingers trace along my inner thighs, purposefully avoiding where I need him to touch me. "Tell me what you want."

I can't. I can't say it out loud.

"I can't," I gasp when he slides one finger inside me, moving it in slow, lazy motions.

"Can't what? Can't tell me you want this?" He adds a second finger, sinking all the way inside me. I instantly arch against the pumpkin, my body instinctively trying to open wider for him. "Can't admit that you want to be absolutely ruined by a masked man in a pumpkin patch?"

Yes. The word echoes in my head, but I refuse to say it.

"Your body is already giving you away," he murmurs, his thumb finding my clit and making me cry out. "You're so tight around my fingers. So desperate. So fucking greedy."

His other hand rips my corset open and squeezes my breast, and the combination of sensations makes my knees tremble. Everything he's doing feels too good, like he knows exactly how and where I want to be touched. Like he knows me.

"You're close already, aren't you?" His voice is rough with arousal now, and I can feel the hard length of him pressed against my hip. "I can feel how you're tightening around me."

I am close—embarrassingly, desperately close. It's like my body is hyperaware of his touch, responding to even the lightest pressure.

"Are you going to come for me again, night monster?" he whispers against my ear. "Show me how greedy that tight cunt is."

His fingers curl inside me at the same time his other hand pinches my nipple, and I break. The orgasm rips through me, stars dancing in my vision amongst the glowing pumpkins.

"Beautiful," he murmurs, smiling down at me with his fingers still inside me, milking out every last drop of my orgasm. "You're so fucking beautiful when you come."

"This time," he says, withdrawing his fingers and making me whimper at the loss. "I want to see how beautiful you are when you come on my cock."

I watch through half-lidded eyes as he reaches for his belt, his movements smooth and unhurried. The sound of leather sliding through his pant loops makes my spine tingle, almost to the point of making me shiver.

He sees something on my face that makes him hesitate, and his hand comes up to cup my face, thumb stroking across my cheek. "You want this, night monster. You want me. I can see it in your eyes."

I do. The realization hits me so hard it would knock me back on my feet if I wasn't pressed against this giant pumpkin. *I want him. I want this dangerous, mysterious masked man to fuck me until I can't see straight.*

"I hate that I want this," I whisper, the words torn from deep inside me. "I hate that my body responds to you. I hate that I don't even want to escape you."

His lips spread across his face slowly, revealing a devilishly handsome smile. "Finally. A little honesty."

I stare back at him, scanning his features. He looks so familiar, but I can't place him.

"I'm going to fuck you now," he says, his voice deepening. "Right here, against these jack-o'-lanterns, with the fog swirling around us and the moon watching from above." His thumbs stroke across my cheekbones. "And you're going to let me, because you want it just as much as I do."

Yes.

"Yes," I whisper, and it feels like stepping off a cliff into free fall.

His smile turns wicked. "Good girl."

He kisses me then, claiming my mouth with his. I kiss him back, desperate and needy and so fucking willing to melt into him.

I know I've lost my mind.

But I don't care anymore. I don't care about anything except the way he's touching me, the way he's making me feel like I'm burning alive with want.

When he finally breaks the kiss, we're both breathing hard. "Turn around," he commands, his voice demanding.

I turn around. There is no hesitation. Because the truth is, I want him to fuck me. To bury his cock so fucking deep inside me I can't think about anything other than the building pressure in my lower stomach.

His hands are on me immediately, pulling my hips out as he frees his dick from his pants. He grunts a few times as he strokes himself, and then lines himself up at my entrance.

A whimper climbs up my throat as he presses into me. I try to suppress it, but it's no use.

My body wants him as badly as he wants me.

He slaps his hand on my ass, making me cry out and arch deeper as the sound echoes through the pumpkin patch.

"Oh god," I breathe when he slides the head of his dick through my folds.

He slides into me gradually, giving me time to adjust to his size, and oh fuck, he's huge. Bigger than I've ever experienced, stretching me until I don't think I can take any more. I brace my hands against the pumpkin in front of me, trying to stay upright as he fills me completely.

"Fuck," he groans, his voice strained. "You feel so fucking good."

He does too. He feels like everything I've been missing, like a piece of myself I didn't know was gone. The thought should scare me, but instead it makes me push back against him, taking him even deeper.

"That's it," he murmurs, his hands gripping my hips. "Let that greedy little pussy swallow my cock."

He starts to move in and out of me, and each thrust makes it impossible to cage the sounds escaping my lips—desperate whimpers and gasps that echo through the fog.

"Fuck," he hisses against my neck, his thrusts increasing in pace and brutality. "I'm gonna fuck you until you can't walk, and then you'll crawl to me on your knees while you beg for my cock to fill you one more time."

His words make me clench around him, and he groans in response, his grip on my hips tightening. The carved faces of the jack-o'-lanterns are all watching us in my peripheral vision, witnesses to my complete surrender to this madness.

But all I feel is pleasure, building and building with each stroke until I can barely breathe.

Thinking becomes impossible when he reaches around and finds my clit with his fingers, rubbing it in tight circles with his thrusts. I'm spiraling toward another orgasm.

"Come on my cock," he commands, his voice rough with his own approaching climax. "Let me feel you fall apart around me."

I do. God help me, I do. I cry out, nearly screaming as I come, meeting each of his brutal thrusts half-way.

"Fuck," I sob, my entire body trembling.

He pounds into me faster, *harder* as he follows me over the edge, his hips stuttering as he finds his own release, roaring into the night.

CHAPTER 6
THE FINAL HUNT

Luke

She's so fucking beautiful when she comes apart for me, her body still trembling against the massive pumpkins as I pull out of her and tuck myself back into my pants. The way she just gave into me completely, the way she *begged* for my cock with every desperate thrust back against me—it's everything I dreamed it would be and more.

My night monster. My obsession.

Mine.

I watch her try to catch her breath, her legs shaking so badly she can barely stand upright. The fake blood from her vampire costume has smeared across her throat and chest, mixing with the sweat from our fucking, and her corset hangs open where I tore it apart to get at her tits. She looks thoroughly claimed, thoroughly ruined, and the sight fills me with a possessive satisfaction so deep it's almost violent.

This is what she was made for. This is what she's always needed.

Someone who'll take her exactly as hard as she craves.

But even as I savor the sight of her completely undone, I can feel the familiar hunger rising in my chest again. It's not enough. It's never going to be enough until she's completely mine, until she understands that this isn't just about one night of fantasy fulfillment.

This is about forever.

This is about her never leaving me.

Every instinct I have is screaming at me to forget the rest of the plan, to just take her right here over and over until she's so broken and desperate she'll agree to anything I ask. But I can't. Not yet. The final act has to be perfect, has to happen exactly where I've planned it.

At the altar I built for her.

Where I'm going to make her mine forever.

I reach into my open shirt and check that the ring is still secure on its chain around my neck. *Soon.* So fucking soon I'll show her what this was really about.

What she's really going to become.

"You did so well, night monster," I murmur, reaching out to pull her bottom lip down with fingers that still smell like her pussy. "But we're not finished yet."

Her eyes flutter open, still glazed with the aftermath of her orgasm, and I can see the confusion and lingering arousal warring in her expression. "What do you mean? How could there possibly be more?"

I mean I'm going to hunt you one more time through my maze, drive you exactly where I want you, and then fuck you on the altar I built while I—

I mean you're never leaving this place as the same woman who entered it.

But I can't tell her that. Not yet. It's not time.

"I mean the night isn't over," I say instead, stepping back and giving her space to pull her torn clothing back together. "We still have the grand finale."

She stares at me like I belong in an asylum, which maybe I

do. Maybe loving someone this desperately, this completely, is a form of insanity.

If it is, I don't want to be cured.

"The grand finale?" Her voice is hoarse from screaming through her orgasms, and the sound makes my cock twitch again. "I can barely stand."

"Then you'd better rest quickly," I say, circling her slowly like the predator I've become. "Because in five minutes, I'm going to hunt you through this patch one last time. And when I catch you—not if, *when*—I'm going to do it somewhere very special."

I can see her trying to process what I'm telling her, her brilliant mind working even through the haze of exhaustion and arousal.

"Where?" she asks, looking around.

"You'll see," I grin beneath my mask, reaching out to brush a strand of hair from her face. The gesture is tender, but my hard eyes never leave hers. "It's at the very heart of everything I've built. The center of my world."

I adjust my devil mask, watching as her pupils dilate at the sight. She's learned to associate this mask with pleasure now, with *surrender*, with the dark parts of herself she's finally allowing to surface.

Perfect.

"Five minutes to catch your breath, night monster," I say, my voice taking on that commanding edge that makes her shiver. "And then you run for me one last time."

And this time, when I catch you, you're never getting away.

I step back into the fog, letting it swallow me so she can't see where I've gone. But I'm watching her. I'm *always* watching her. Learning her patterns, memorizing every micro-expression, cataloging every tell that shows me what she's really thinking.

She's not going to run toward the forest this time.

She's going to run deeper into my field of pumpkins, because part of her wants to see what else I've built for her.

Part of her wants to be caught by me again.

Part of her is already mine, even if she doesn't consciously understand it yet.

I use the time to position myself strategically, calculating the angles and pathways that will drive her exactly where I need her to go. The altar I've constructed is at the highest point of the patch, surrounded by the most elaborate jack-o'-lanterns and hidden until the last possible moment by carefully positioned fog machines.

I can't wait for her to see it.

My heart is pounding harder than it has all night with the anticipation and nerves I'm trying to push down. This is it. This is the moment when everything comes together.

She's going to be mine.

She has to be mine.

Because I've already decided she's never leaving me.

"Time's up," I call through the fog, my voice echoing off the surrounding forest and carrying through the thick mist. "Start running."

I hear her gasp, then the sound of her feet hitting the soft earth as she bolts deeper into the field. Exactly as I predicted. Exactly as I planned.

My brilliant girl.

Running straight into my trap.

I count to thirty, then begin my final pursuit. But this isn't like the other chases. This time I'm not just hunting her— I'm *herding* her, using my knowledge of the field's layout to cut off every escape route except the one that leads to where I need her.

To the altar.

To our future.

The fog is thickest here, rolling in waves that make the jack-o'-lanterns appear and disappear like they're from a fever dream. I can hear her ahead of me, stumbling through the vines, and every sound she makes sends electricity through my veins.

Soon.

So fucking soon.

I drive her left when she tries to go right, block her path when she attempts to double back, and use my superior knowledge of this place to eliminate every option except forward momentum.

Deeper into my web.

Closer to where this all ends.

Where this all begins.

She's getting tired—I can hear it in her breathing, in the way her footsteps are becoming less coordinated. Perfect. I want her exhausted when she reaches our final destination. I want her desperate and confused and completely dependent on me.

I want her to have no choice but to surrender to whatever I offer her.

The pathways are narrowing now, funneling her toward the single entrance that leads to the best part of it all. I can hear her starting to panic as she realizes she's being driven right where I want her.

It's too late to turn back now, baby.

You can't escape what we're going to become.

I emerge from the fog just close enough for her to see me, to know I'm right behind her, and hear her sob with exhaustion and terror and...

Anticipation.

She *wants* to see what's waiting for her at the end.

She wants to know what I've been building toward all night.

The entrance to the altar appears ahead of us through the fog—an archway made of intertwined pumpkin vines and late-autumn flowers, lit from within by dozens of candles and positioned so she'll have to stop and stare before she can enter.

Before she can see what I've prepared for her.

Before she can understand what this was always really about.

I hang back, letting her approach the entrance alone, watching as she comes to a complete stop at the threshold.

Perfect.

Absolutely fucking perfect.

She's right where I want her.

Exactly where she's always belonged.

Now all that's left is to show her what forever looks like.

CHAPTER 7
HALLOWEEN QUEEN

Seraphina

I'm standing at the entrance to what looks like it was torn straight from a dark fairy tale, and I can't breathe.

The archway before me is made of intertwined pumpkin vines and deep purple flowers, lit from within by dozens of flickering candles that cast dancing shadows through the fog. Beyond it, I can see what looks like a stage—an elevated platform surrounded by the most elaborate jack-o'-lanterns I've seen yet, each one carved with intricate designs that seem to move in the candlelight.

What is this?

My legs are shaking from exhaustion and adrenaline, my body still sensitive from the way he fucked me against those pumpkins. I know I should be running, trying to escape into the forest, to find help, to get as far away from this beautiful madman as possible...

But I can't move. I'm frozen at this threshold, staring at whatever elaborate scene he's constructed at the heart of his plan.

He did all of this... for me?

The thought makes my head spin. The magnitude of what I'm looking at—the stage, the candles, the perfectly positioned jack-o'-lanterns—this is months of work. Maybe longer.

But why?

My feet are already carrying me forward, through the archway and toward the stage. I can't help myself. I need to see what's up there, to understand why he's doing all of this.

Stone steps lead up to the platform, carved from dark granite and lined with more flickering candles. I climb them slowly, my boots silent on the smooth stone, and as I reach the top, my breath catches in my throat.

Oh my God.

The stage is draped in black silk that pools and flows like water in the candlelight. Black rose petals are scattered across every surface, and in the center sits a bed—an actual fucking bed with a plush mattress covered in more black silk and pillows.

This is easily the most beautiful thing I've ever seen. Gothic and romantic and terrifying all at once.

I walk further onto the stage, my fingers trailing over the silk draping. It's real silk, expensive and smooth against my skin. Everything here looks expensive.

That's when I see it.

On a pedestal near the bed, sitting on a cushion of black velvet, is a crown. Not some cheap costume jewelry, but a real crown made of obsidian and gold, with intricate metalwork that catches the candlelight and throws it back in mesmerizing patterns.

A *crown*.

He built me a throne room and put a crown in it.

What kind of game is this?

My hand is reaching for it before I can stop myself, fingers hovering just inches from the gold. It's beautiful. It drips *power*.

"It suits you."

I spin around to find him standing at the top of the steps, having followed me up here with that same predatory grace. The devil mask is still in place, but I can see his eyes through the openings, and they're burning with an intensity that makes my knees weak.

"I don't understand," I say, backing away from the crown like it might bite me. "What is this?"

"This," he says, walking toward me with slow, deliberate steps, "is where everything changes."

His vague answer only confuses me more.

"Where what changes?" I raise an eyebrow at him, feeling too comfortable in this space with him. "I'm nobody to you. We don't even know each other."

"You're wrong," he says simply, reaching the pedestal and picking up the crown. "You're so much more than you've let yourself believe."

No. No, this is crazy. This is all crazy.

But I can't look away from the crown in his hands, can't stop imagining what it would feel like to wear something so beautiful, so powerful.

"You're a queen, night monster," he murmurs, stepping closer. "My queen. And it's time you understood that."

His queen.

I'm screaming internally. What does that even mean?

Before I can protest, before I can think clearly enough to move away, he's behind me, lifting the crown toward my head.

"No," I whisper, but it comes out too softly.

"Yes," he disagrees, and settles the crown on my head.

The weight of it is immediate and profound, like it's changing my entire center of gravity. The metal is cold against my scalp, and I can feel power radiating from it—or maybe that's just my imagination.

Fuck.

It feels *right*. Like it belongs on my head.

"It's perfect," he breathes, his hands settling on my shoulders as he turns me to face the bed. "Absolutely fucking perfect."

I imagine what I look like to him right now—a woman in a torn vampire costume wearing a crown of obsidian and gold, standing in a gothic temple surrounded by black silk and candlelight.

I look like a dark queen.

I look like someone who belongs in a place as wicked and sinister as this pumpkin patch.

I look like someone who could rule beside a monster as beautiful and possessive as *him*.

"Now," he says, his voice taking on that commanding edge that makes my back arch instinctively, "let me worship my queen properly."

His hands are on me before I can process what he means, gentle but insistent as he guides me toward the bed.

I should fight him and demand answers. And I know I should ask him who the fuck he is and why he's done all this...

But I don't. I let him lead me to the silk-covered mattress, help me climb onto it, arrange me among the black rose petals like I'm the finishing touch in his art piece.

Like I'm something worth worshipping.

The crown shifts slightly as I move, but it doesn't fall. It stays balanced on my head, like it was made specifically for me.

Was it?

Did he have this crown made for me specifically?

How long has he been planning this?

"Lie back," he says as he nudges me back, and I do, sinking

into silk and rose petals and the most comfortable mattress I've ever felt.

His hands are everywhere—stroking over my skin, spreading my legs wide as he kneels between them. The devil mask looks even more dramatic in the brighter candlelight. It's demonic beauty.

He's going to eat me alive.

And I'm going to let him.

"Such a beautiful Halloween queen," he growls, running his hands up my thighs. "Such a perfect fucking queen."

I arch beneath his touch, already desperate for more. My body is learning to crave him, to respond to his voice and his hands with an eagerness that should shame me but doesn't.

Not when he has me like this.

Wearing his crown and sprawled out over the most expensive silks.

He reaches beneath the pillow beside my head and pulls out something that makes me blink in confusion—a vibrator, but not just any vibrator. It's shaped like candy corn, orange and yellow and white, and it's the most ridiculous thing I've ever seen.

A candy corn vibrator.

He brought a fucking candy corn vibrator to his gothic sex altar.

I recognize the absolute insanity of this situation, but I start to laugh. It bubbles up from my chest before I can stop it, and once I start, I can't seem to stop.

"You think this is funny?" he asks, but there's amusement in his voice too.

"It's Halloween-themed," I gasp between laughs. "Of course it's Halloween-themed. Of course you have a candy corn vibrator."

This beautiful madman planned everything down to seasonal sex toys.

"I'm thorough," he says with a grin I can hear in his voice. "And I thought my queen should have something appropriately festive."

His queen.

He keeps calling me his queen.

And I keep letting him.

The laughter dies in my throat as he turns the vibrator on, the soft buzzing sound mixing with the Halloween music still playing in the background. He traces it over my inner thighs, not quite touching where I need him most, and I'm instantly on fire again.

Fuck.

How does he do this to me?

"Please," I whisper, and there's no shame in it anymore. No embarrassment. Just need.

"Please what, my queen?" he asks, still teasing me with the ridiculous vibrator.

"Please touch me," I breathe. "Please make me come. Please don't stop."

Please don't ever stop.

Please keep me here in this dark fairy tale forever.

"Since you asked so nicely," he murmurs, and presses the vibrator against my clit.

I cry out, my back lifting off the silk as pleasure shoots through me. The setting is perfect—not too intense, not too gentle, just exactly what I need right now. And the fact that it's shaped like candy corn makes it even more arousing, like he's claiming me with Halloween itself.

His hands, his voice, his ridiculous seasonal sex toys.

Everything about this man is claiming me. And I *want* to be his.

He works me with the vibrator and his fingers, building me up slowly this time, drawing out every moan until I'm trembling and begging and completely lost to the pleasure.

"That's it," he says, watching my face with those intense green eyes. "Come for your king, my queen."

My king.

He thinks he's my king and I'm his queen and this is our dark kingdom.

I shatter around his fingers, the crown shifting on my head as I throw it back and scream for him into the night. The orgasm explodes, and I cling to the sheets like I'm desperately trying to hold onto reality.

As I come down, he's still kneeling between my legs, still watching me with that possessive gaze.

I need more.

I need *all* of him.

"I want to ride you," I hear myself say, the words tumbling out before I can stop them. "I want to fuck you while I wear your crown."

His eyes flash with hunger. "Then take what you want, my queen."

He lies back on the silk, pulling me up to straddle him as he frees his cock from his pants. I can see all of him now—

the tattoos across his chest, the way his muscles flex as he moves, the perfect masculinity of him beneath me.

My king.

My beautiful, dangerous king.

I sink down onto him slowly, savoring every inch as he fills me completely. The crown is heavy on my head, reminding me with every movement that I'm his queen, that this is my throne, that he's made me into something powerful and dark and absolutely *his*.

This is where I belong. As fucked up as it may seem to literally anyone else, this is who I am.

I start to move, riding him with increasing desperation as he grips my hips and helps guide my movements. The silk slides beneath us, the candles flicker around us, and the crown stays perfectly balanced on my head like it was always meant to be there.

"Fuck," he groans, his head falling back as I take him deeper. "Don't stop."

Now he's the one begging me to keep going. I feel a sense of pride, like I've somehow gained an ounce of control in this situation.

I'm close again, the pleasure building with every roll of my hips, every flex of his hands on my skin. I can feel him getting close too, in the way his jaw clenches beneath the mask, in the way his breathing gets ragged.

"Come with me," I demand, using the voice of a queen giving orders to her king. "Fill me with your cum until I can't take any more. I want your seed dripping out of me."

He does, roaring loudly as he empties himself inside me, and I follow him over the edge, my crown shifting but never falling as I collapse against his chest.

We lie there panting under the moon, my body draped over his, our limbs tangled in a sticky mess.

That's when I see *it*.

A glint of metal against his throat, half-hidden by his open shirt. Something small and round hanging from a chain around his neck.

What is that?

I lift my head slightly, trying to get a better look, and my breath catches. My heart stops.

It looks like...

CHAPTER 8
PUMPKIN PATCH PROPOSAL

Seraphina

A white gold ring glints in the candlelight, and my entire world stops spinning.

A ring.

A fucking engagement ring hanging around his neck. How did I not notice?

I scramble off of him so fast I nearly fall off the bed, the crown tumbling from my head as I stare at him in shock. My legs are shaking, my heart hammering against my ribs.

Oh my god.

Oh my *fucking* god.

"Luke?" The name falls from my lips, and I've instantly broken out of character.

He grins as he sits up slowly, reaching for the chain around his neck, and when he pulls off the devil mask with his other hand, I see the face I've known for the past two years. The face I wake up next to every morning. The face of the man I'm completely, utterly in love with.

Luke.

My Luke.

I thought we were only here to roleplay my kidnapping and primal play fantasy.

But *this*...

This is...

"Luke, are you serious?" I gasp, pointing at the ring he's now holding as tears form in my eyes. "Is this real?"

His smile is soft and nervous, but he nods. "I'm serious."

"You did all of this to propose to me?" My voice is climbing toward hysteria. "*All* of this? The entire pumpkin patch, the hunting, the stage, the crown—you did all of this because you want to *marry* me?"

"Not just because I want to marry you," he says gently, sitting up and reaching for me. "Because I can't live without you. Because you're everything I've ever wanted and everything I never knew I needed."

I can't breathe.

I literally cannot breathe.

"Luke," I whisper, sinking down onto the silk beside him. "When we planned tonight, you never said anything about —I thought we were just acting out my fantasy. I had no idea you've been planning all of this."

"It was about roleplaying," he says, his eyes never leaving mine. "But it was also so much more than that. Sera, you told me about wanting to be chased through a pumpkin patch by someone who wanted you desperately enough to burn the world for you." His voice drops, becoming softer, more vulnerable. "So I became that person. I literally became someone who would move mountains to possess you. I want to burn the world for you, and then rebuild it exactly how you want it."

Move mountains.

He moved actual mountains. He rearranged a fucking forest to build this pumpkin patch for me.

"How long have you been planning this?" I'm still shocked, wide-eyed and stunned as I look around us. My heart won't stop pounding.

"Fifteen months," he admits. "From the moment you told me about that book you read. From the moment I saw how your eyes lit up when you described being hunted and claimed."

Fifteen months. He's been planning this for fifteen months. And I had no idea. How clueless am I?

"You built me a pumpkin patch in the middle of a forest," I say, trying to hold back the tears. "You actually built me a pumpkin patch and had hundreds of pumpkins carved and got fog machines... You created an entire fantasy world because I mentioned liking a book."

"Because I love you," he says simply. "Because you deserve someone who will make your wildest dreams come true. Because you're worth every penny I spent, every hour I planned, every detail I obsessed over."

Every detail.

The seasonal sex toys, the crown, the gothic sex altar.

He planned *everything*.

"Luke Morrison," I say, my voice shaking through my smile. "You are completely insane."

"Insanely in love with you," he agrees, sliding off the bed and onto one knee in the silk and rose petals. "Which brings me to why we're here."

He's actually doing it.

He's actually proposing to me on a gothic altar in the middle of a pumpkin patch. This is the most thoughtful proposal of all time. Every dark romance and erotic horror reader's dream come to life.

The sight of him holding the ring, down on one knee makes the tears fall from my eyes. I can't stop them as they slide down my cheeks.

It's beautiful.

It's the most beautiful thing I've ever seen.

And it's exactly what I would have chosen for myself.

"Seraphina," he begins, his voice rough with emotion. "Two years ago, you walked into my life and completely destroyed every plan I had for my future. You made me want things I never thought I'd want. You made me become someone I never thought I could be."

Oh god.

I'm sobbing now, letting the tears free fall onto the silk below us.

"You are brilliant and fierce and secretly wild in ways that take my breath away," he continues. "You deserve a man who will build you worlds where your deepest fantasies can come true. You deserve someone who will love every dark, beautiful corner of your soul."

He *does* love every corner of my soul.

Including the parts that want to be hunted through pumpkin patches by masked men.

"I promise to keep hunting you for the rest of our lives," Luke says, and I can see tears gathering in his green eyes. "I promise to keep surprising you, keep challenging you, keep making you feel desired and treasured and absolutely essential to my existence."

Yes.

God, *yes.*

"I promise to build you new adventures every year, to never let our love become predictable or ordinary," he continues. "I promise to love your darkness as much as your light, your wildness as much as your tenderness, your secrets as much as your truths."

He's killing me. This is beyond my wildest dreams.

"And I promise that no matter how many years we have together, I will never stop being amazed that somehow, *impossibly*, you chose to be caught by *me*."

Caught by him. Forever.

That's exactly what I want.

To be caught by Luke Morrison.

"Seraphina Williams," he begins, and my chest tightens. "Will you marry me?"

Yes.

Before the words even make it out of my mouth, I'm launching myself at him with enough force to knock him backward into the silk. I plaster his face with kisses, tasting my happy tears combining with his.

"Yes," I say between kisses. "Yes, yes, *yes*, you beautiful, insane, perfect man."

Yes to everything.

Yes to marrying him, yes to spending my life with someone who would build me a haunted forest just to propose, yes to whatever incredible adventure comes next.

He slides the ring onto my finger with hands that are shaking almost as much as mine, and it fits perfectly. Of course it fits perfectly. This is Luke we're talking about. He probably had my ring size secretly measured while I was sleeping.

The ring is gorgeous. It's absolutely stunning.

And it's mine.

I'm *engaged*.

"I love you," I tell him, cupping his face in my hands. "I love you so much it scares me sometimes. But this... Luke, this was the most incredible thing anyone has ever done for anyone in the history of the world."

"I love you too," he says, pulling me down for another kiss. "More than anything."

I grin against his lips, settling against his chest in the silk and rose petals. The crown has fallen onto the bed, but I don't need it anymore. I already feel like a queen just being loved by him.

This is my life now.

"So what happens now?" I ask, admiring the way my new ring catches the moonlight.

"Now," Luke says, his voice taking on that familiar edge that makes my pulse race, "I was thinking we could celebrate our engagement *properly*."

Oh.

Oh my.

I look down and realize he's already getting hard again beneath me, his cock pressing against my thigh. The combination of proposal endorphins and the lingering adrenaline from our chase is making me feel reckless and wild and absolutely desperate for him.

I want to celebrate... By worshipping my fiancé the way he deserves.

"I have an idea," I say, sliding off of him and onto my knees between his thighs. "Let me show you how grateful I am for the most perfect proposal in history."

His eyes darken as he realizes what I'm offering. "Sera..."

"I want to taste you," I tell him, reaching for his zipper. "I want to suck my fiancé's cock on our engagement altar."

My life is absolutely insane and I fucking love it.

His breath catches as I work his dick free. My mouth is already watering just thinking about tasting him, about showing him with my lips and tongue how much I love him, how grateful I am for everything he's done.

My fiancé.

I get to call him my fiancé now.

And soon, my husband.

I smile up at him as I bite at my bottom lip, ready to show him exactly how much I appreciate his pumpkin patch proposal.

CHAPTER 9
BEYOND THE CHASE

Luke

S he's on her knees before me, and I can barely breathe from how fucking perfect she looks.

The engagement ring catches the candlelight as she reaches for my cock, the diamond throwing rainbow fractals across her face in the flickering glow. My ring. My fiancée. *My* future wife kneeling on the altar I built for us, desperate to celebrate our engagement with her mouth on my cock.

This is everything I've ever wanted.

It's everything I never dared dream I could have.

"Fuck, Sera," I breathe as she takes me in her hand and begins pumping me. "You look so fucking beautiful wearing my ring."

She glances up at me through her lashes, and her dark expression makes my head spin. "Your ring," she murmurs, pressing a soft kiss to the head of my cock.

Mine. Completely, utterly, irrevocably *mine.*

The possessive feeling that floods through me is so intense it's almost violent. She said yes. She's wearing my ring. She's going to be Seraphina Morrison, and every man who looks at her will know she's taken.

"That's right," I growl, threading my fingers through her hair and letting out a low groan.

She hums her agreement against my skin, the vibration making me twitch in her hand. Then she's taking me into her mouth, and rational thought becomes impossible.

Holy fuck.

Her tongue is warm and wet as it swirls around the head of my cock, tasting me like I'm her final meal. She takes me deeper, inch by inch, until I can feel myself hitting the back of her throat.

My perfect, filthy, night monster. Taking my cock like she owns it.

She *does* own it. Every part of me belongs to her. Mind, body, and soul. It's all for her.

"God, baby," I groan, fighting to keep my hips from bucking too hard as she pumps herself over my cock. "Your mouth feels so fucking good."

She pulls off just long enough to look up at me with those beautiful blue eyes, lips swollen and wet from sucking me. "I want to taste you," she says, her voice husky with arousal. "I want to swallow everything you give me. I want you to come in my mouth."

Fuck.

My hips jerk as her fingers tease the head of my cock.

She's going to kill me.

She takes me back into her mouth, deeper this time, and I can feel her throat working around the head of my cock as she fights her gag reflex. The sight of her struggling to take all of me, determined to please me even when it's difficult, makes something primal and possessive roar to life in my chest.

That's my girl, taking everything I give her and desperate for more.

I can't help but think about how we got here, about the months of planning that led to this moment. Every detail I obsessed over, every contingency I planned for, every dollar I spent—all of it came to this. Her on her knees in front of me with my ring on her finger and my cock in her mouth.

Worth every fucking penny.

Worth every sleepless night.

She's found her rhythm now, taking me deep and pulling back, using her tongue to trace patterns along my shaft that make my vision blur. The wet sounds of her mouth working me fill the air, mixing with the Halloween music still playing in the background and the distant howl of wolves.

It's the sound of my fiancée worshipping my cock on the altar I built for her.

I look down at her—*really* look—and the sight nearly undoes me. Her dark hair is messed up from my fingers, her vampire makeup smeared and running from tears and exertion. The torn corset hangs open, giving me glimpses of her perfect tits as she bobs. And on her finger, catching the light with every stroke of her hand, is my ring.

My mark.

My claim.

My promise that she'll never belong to anyone else.

"You look so fucking beautiful like this," I tell her, my voice rough with arousal and emotion. "On your knees for me, wearing my ring, taking my cock like the perfect little queen you are."

She moans around me, the vibration making my head fall back and my hand tighten around her hair. Her free hand comes up to cup my balls, rolling them gently in her palm while she continues to suck me with an enthusiasm that borders on worship.

She loves this. She loves being on her knees for me, belonging to me as much as I love owning her.

The thought sends heat racing through my veins, and I can feel my orgasm building at the base of my spine. But I don't want this to end. I want to stay in this moment forever.

"Such a good girl," I murmur, holding her head still while I begin thrusting into her, fucking her face. "Such a perfect, *filthy*, gorgeous girl. Taking my cock so well. You like it when I fuck your face, don't you?"

She tries to pull off to catch her breath, still stroking me with both hands and looking up at me with lust-dark eyes, but I don't let her. Her eyes widen, but I take that as my opportunity to push deeper, to make her lose control and gag. Saliva runs down the side of her mouth.

"You've always been mine," I tell her, pumping into her. "From the first night we met, you've belonged to me."

She relaxes and takes me deep again. She works her throat around me, swallowing me down like she's trying to take every inch I have to give. The sight of her struggling to accommodate my size, tears streaming down her cheeks but never giving up, makes me even harder.

That's it, baby.

Take everything.

I can feel myself getting close, my balls tightening as she continues her relentless assault on my self-control. The combination of her hot mouth, her wet tongue, and the sight of my ring glittering on her finger is too much.

I'm going to come down her throat.

I'm going to fill her dirty little mouth and make her swallow every drop.

"Sera," I warn, my voice strained. "Baby, I'm close."

She doesn't pull away. If anything, she doubles her efforts, sucking harder, taking me deeper, using both hands to stroke what doesn't fit in her mouth. She *wants* this. She wants me to come for her, wants to taste my surrender the way I've tasted hers all night.

This is all so fucking perfect.

I lose control and I come hard, filling her mouth with pulse after pulse while she swallows everything I give her, her throat working around my cock as she takes it all.

When I finally stop shaking, she pulls off slowly, licking me clean with gentle strokes of her tongue. Then she sits back on her heels, looking up at me with satisfaction and love shining in her eyes.

I sink to my knees in front of her, framing her face with my hands and kissing her deeply. I can taste myself on her lips, can feel the slight roughness in her throat from taking me so deep, and it makes me want to propose to her all over again.

She said yes.

She's going to marry me.

When we finally break apart, I take her left hand in mine, bringing it to my lips to press a gentle kiss to the ring I placed there. The diamond sparkles in the moonlight, beautiful and perfect and exactly what she deserves.

I look up at her, meeting her eyes as I kiss the ring one more time.

"Happy Halloween, night monster."

EPILOGUE 1
WINTER WONDERLAND

Seraphina

Over One Year Later - December 22nd

I'm walking down an aisle made of evergreen boughs and white roses, and I can't stop smiling.

The same property where Luke built his elaborate pumpkin patch maze has been transformed into the most magical winter wedding venue I could've imagined. Where once there were jack-o'-lanterns casting eerie shadows in the fog, now there are towering pine trees wrapped in thousands of twinkling fairy lights that sparkle like stars against the December evening sky. The pathways that I once ran through in terror are now lined with red rose petals and glowing lanterns that cast a warm, golden light across the snow-covered ground.

A little more than a year ago, I was running through this same space in a sexy vampire costume.

Today, I'm walking through it in my wedding dress, about to marry the man of my dreams.

The transformation is breathtaking. Luke has kept the basic magic of this place—the winding pathways, the sense of entering another world, the theatrical atmosphere that makes everything feel like stepping into a fairy tale—but everything else has been reimagined for romance rather than fear. Instead of ominous fog, delicate snow falls gently from the sky, catching in my hair and on my dress like nature's own confetti. Instead of Halloween music, a string quartet plays softly from a gazebo draped in white silk and winter greenery.

My father squeezes my arm as we navigate around a particularly elaborate ice sculpture—a pair of intertwined hearts that sparkle in the fairy lights. "You sure about this one, kiddo? It's never too late to back out and be my little girl forever."

I laugh, remembering how much running I did in this very spot over a year ago. "I'm done running, Dad. I found exactly what I was looking for."

The guests are seated on deep red chairs arranged throughout the winter wonderland, following the natural curves of the pathways. Luke insisted that everyone experience the full journey through his creation, so instead of traditional rows facing an altar, our friends and family are positioned at various points along the route to the center. Each group gets a different perspective of the ceremony, like scenes in a play unfolding as I make my way through the field.

I can see some of our friends from college near the first turn, bundled in elegant winter coats and taking pictures as I pass. My coworkers from the accounting firm are clustered around one of the larger ice sculptures, looking stunned by the magic of it all. Luke's business partners are positioned near what used to be the section where he first caught me, and I feel my cheeks warm as I remember what happened there...

"Nervous?" Dad asks as we approach the final turn before the clearing.

"Not even a little bit," I answer honestly.

We round the final corner, and the space opens up before us like something out of a winter fairy tale. The same space where Luke proposed is now decorated with towering evergreen trees wrapped in fairy lights, with an arch made of intertwined pine boughs and white roses.

Battery-powered candles create pools of warm golden light throughout the gently falling snow, and overhead, more string lights stretch between the trees like stars.

It's perfect.

It's absolutely perfect.

And there he is, standing beneath the floral arch in his perfectly tailored black tuxedo, looking at me like I'm the most beautiful thing he's ever seen. His green eyes are bright with unshed tears, and that smile—that devastating smile—is radiant with joy.

The sight of him hits me with a wave of emotion so intense I have to pause for a moment to catch my breath. Dad steadies me with a gentle hand on my elbow.

"Second thoughts?" he whispers the joke, smiling down at me through kind eyes.

"Never," I whisper back, my voice shaking as I fight to hold back the tears. I can't ruin my makeup. "I'm just... I'm so happy, Dad. I'm so incredibly, overwhelmingly happy."

As we near the end of the aisle, I take in all the familiar faces surrounding us. Our families, our friends, everyone we love most in the world is here to witness this moment. Despite being surrounded by nearly four hundred people, it still feels intimate and private.

Luke's best man, his brother David, grins at me from beside the arch, his breath creating small puffs of steam in the cold air. Luke's parents are seated in the front row, his mother already dabbing at her eyes with a handkerchief. My own mother is practically vibrating with excitement.

The secret knowledge of how this place came to be makes me feel even more connected to Luke, like we're sharing a private joke that no one else understands. Which, in a way, we are.

Dad places my hand in Luke's with the traditional words about giving me away, but I barely hear them. I'm too busy staring into Luke's green eyes.

"Hi," Luke whispers, taking both my hands in his.

"Hi," I whisper back, and suddenly it's like everyone else disappears. There's just him and me and the magical space he created for us.

The officiant—the same friend of Luke's from college who got ordained online specifically for this ceremony—begins speaking words about love and commitment and joining together. But I'm only half listening, too caught up in the surreal perfection of this moment.

"The bride and groom have chosen to write their own vows," the officiant announces, and Luke pulls out a folded piece of paper from his jacket pocket.

Of course he wrote vows. He's too organized not to. I tear up at the thought alone. He's so fucking thoughtful.

"Seraphina," Luke begins, his voice steady despite the tears I can see gathering in his eyes. "Just over one year ago, I asked you to marry me in this very spot. But the truth is, I've been working toward asking you that question every day since the moment we met."

Oh God.

He's going to make me cry before he even gets started.

"Every surprise I've planned, every world I've built for you, every moment I've spent loving you has been my way of asking if you'll stay with me forever," he continues. "Every time I've shown you a new side of yourself, I've been asking if you'll trust me to keep exploring those depths with you."

He's right.

"You are brilliant and passionate and beautifully wild in ways that take my breath away," Luke says, his voice growing stronger even though the tears in his eyes are swelling. "You deserve a man who will create magic for you, who will love every corner of your soul, who will spend his life making sure you never doubt how extraordinary you are."

"I promise to keep surprising you for the rest of our lives," Luke says. "I promise to keep building you adventures, to never let our love become predictable or ordinary, to always remember that loving you means loving your wildest dreams too."

Yes. I nod at him, trying so hard to hold back my emotions.

God, yes.

The officiant turns to me expectantly, and I pull out my own folded paper, though my hands are shaking so badly I can barely unfold it.

Okay, Sera. Don't cry. Don't completely lose it in front of four hundred people.

Just tell him how you feel.

"Luke," I begin, my voice tight. "When people ask me what makes our love special, I tell them it's because you don't just listen to what I say—you pay attention to what makes my eyes light up. You notice the little things that bring me joy, and somehow you turn those moments into the most incredible surprises," I continue, relaxing slightly. "You have this gift for taking something I mentioned loving and creating an experience around it that's beyond anything I could have imagined."

Like turning a conversation about a book into the most elaborate proposal in history.

"Most men would say 'I love you' with flowers or jewelry," I say, my voice growing stronger. "But you say 'I love you' by creating entire worlds where we can make the most beautiful memories together. You've shown me that love isn't just about finding someone who accepts you as you are—it's about finding someone who sees your dreams and makes them bigger and more beautiful than you ever thought possible."

I pause to wipe the tears from my eyes before they have a chance to fall down my face.

"I promise to keep dreaming big with you, to never stop believing in the magic you create for us," I continue. "I promise to match your creativity with my own adventures, to surprise you as much as you surprise me."

"And I promise to love your generous, thoughtful, wonderfully romantic heart exactly as it is," I finish. "Because a man who turns ordinary moments into fairy tales is exactly the kind of man I want to spend forever with."

Forever in whatever beautiful madness we create together.

The rest of the ceremony passes in a blur of rings and

kisses and "I do's" and finally, *finally*, the words I've been waiting to hear:

"You may kiss your bride."

Luke's kiss is soft and sweet and full of promise, nothing like the desperate, claiming kisses from our night in the pumpkin patch. This is different—this is the kiss of a man who knows he has forever to love me, who doesn't need to rush because I'm never going anywhere.

When we finally break apart, the winter wonderland erupts in cheers and applause. Snow continues to fall from overhead and the fairy lights twinkle around us like something magical and ethereal.

We did it.

We're married.

As we make our way back through the winter field—this time as husband and wife—I can't help but marvel at how perfect everything turned out. The same pathways that once filled me with terror are now filled with the laughter and congratulations of everyone we love. The same clearing where I once surrendered to a masked man is now the site of the most important moment of my life.

EPILOGUE 2
TO THE TREE FARM

Luke

Later that night.

The reception is winding down, and I can barely contain my excitement as I watch my wife —*my wife*—accept final congratulations from our guests. She looks radiant in her wedding dress, the lights from our winter wonderland catching in her hair and making her look like an absolute goddess.

Mrs. Seraphina Morrison.

I've been waiting for this moment all night—hell, I've been waiting for this moment for months. Ever since I started planning the Christmas tree farm, I've been dying to show it to her. The wedding was perfect, absolutely everything I hoped it would be, but this... this is what I'm really excited about.

My wedding gift to her.

The next chapter in our story.

The next world I've built for us to explore together.

She catches my eye across the reception tent and smiles that radiant smile that made me fall in love with her in the first place. I crook my finger at her, and she excuses herself from the conversation she's having with my aunt, making her way over to me with that graceful walk that always makes my heart skip.

"Hello, husband," she says when she reaches me, standing on her toes to press a soft kiss to my lips.

Husband.

I'm never going to get tired of hearing that.

"Hello, *wife*," I reply, wrapping my arms around her waist. "Ready for your wedding present?"

Her eyes light up with curiosity and excitement. "You got me a wedding present? Luke, the winter wonderland wedding was already more than enough."

Oh, baby. You have no idea what I've done.

"The wedding was just the beginning," I tell her, taking her hand and leading her toward the edge of the reception tent. "I have something to show you."

"Luke Morrison," she says, using that tone that means she's both exasperated and charmed by me. "What did you do now?"

Built you another world. Created another adventure for us to share. Spent the last several months designing the perfect Christmas surprise.

"You'll see," I say, helping her into the warm winter coat I had specially made to go over her wedding dress. "But we need to take a little walk first."

She looks at me suspiciously but doesn't protest as I lead her away from the reception tent and toward the tree line. Snow is falling gently around us, creating a perfect winter wonderland atmosphere that makes everything feel magical and surreal.

Perfect timing, as always.

Even Mother Nature is cooperating with my plans tonight.

"Luke, where are we going?" Seraphina asks as we enter the forest, our footsteps crunching softly in the snow. "My dress is going to get ruined."

"Trust me," I say, squeezing her hand gently. "Your dress is going to be ruined by the time I'm done with you."

The thought goes straight to my cock, making it strain against my tux pants.

The forest is beautiful in the moonlight, the snow-covered branches creating a canopy of white lace above our heads. I've walked this path dozens of times over the past few months, supervising the construction, checking every detail, making sure everything would be perfect for this moment.

For her.

It's *always* for her.

"This is beautiful," Seraphina says, her breath creating small puffs of steam in the cold air. "But Luke, seriously, what's going on?"

"Do you remember what you said to me last Christmas?" I ask instead of answering directly. "About how you'd always wanted to get lost in a Christmas tree farm? About how romantic it would be to walk through rows of evergreens under the stars?"

She stops walking, turning to stare at me with wide eyes. "Luke. You didn't."

I did.

I absolutely did.

"I might have," I say with a grin, continuing to lead her through the forest. "We're almost there."

The excitement is practically vibrating through me now. I can see the glow through the trees up ahead—the thousands of lights I had installed throughout the tree farm, the magical candyland atmosphere I spent months creating.

She's going to love it.

"Luke, you are completely insane," Seraphina says, but she's laughing as she says it. "What am I going to do with you?"

Love me forever.

Say *yes* to whatever adventure I plan next.

"Love me forever?" I suggest, bringing her hand to my lips to press a kiss to her wedding ring.

"Always," she says without hesitation. "But Luke, if you've actually built me a Christmas tree farm—"

"Built, bought, and transformed into something absolutely surreal," I confirm, unable to keep the pride out of my voice. "Just wait until you see what I've done with it. You loved being chased through the pumpkin patch, so I figured you'd love being fucked in Christmas tree farm just as much."

We're almost there now. I can see the edge of the forest just ahead, and I can see the first hints of the wonderland I've created for her. My heart is pounding with anticipation and nerves and the same excitement I felt the night I proposed.

We reach the tree line, and I pause for a moment, savoring this last second before we begin the next fantasy.

"Ready?" I ask, though I'm not sure who I'm asking—her or myself.

She nods, her eyes bright with excitement and trust and love.

Here we go.

We step out of the forest together, and Seraphina gasps, bringing her hands to cover her mouth.

Stretched out before us is the most magical Christmas tree farm imaginable. Thousands of evergreen trees arranged in perfect rows, each one wrapped in twinkling lights that create rivers of gold and silver and rainbow colors flowing through the snow. Candy cane-striped posts mark the pathways between the rows, and scattered throughout the farm are elaborate gingerbread houses, candy sculptures, and winter decorations that make the whole place look like something out of a dream.

A magical candyland mixed with a Christmas tree farm.

They say money can't buy happiness... But money can buy *this*...

"Oh my God," Seraphina breathes, her eyes shooting back to me. "Luke, this is... how did you... when did you..."

I wrap my arms around her from behind as we stand at the edge of our next adventure. "The same team that built the pumpkin patch maze and the winter wonderland designed this. It's twenty acres of Christmas magic, just for us."

She leans back against my chest, and I can feel her trembling with excitement. "You built me a Christmas tree farm."

"I built *us* a Christmas tree farm," I correct. "Our next playground. Our next adventure."

"Luke Morrison," she says, turning in my arms to look at me with tears of joy in her eyes. "I love you so much it actually hurts sometimes."

"I love you too," I tell her, pressing a soft kiss to her forehead. "More than words can say."

But I'm going to keep trying.

I'm going to keep building her worlds and making her dreams come true for the rest of our lives.

She looks back at the magical candyland I've created for her, at the thousands of twinkling lights and the snow-covered wonderland stretching out before us.

"So," she says, a wicked smile spreading across her face. "What exactly did you have in mind for our first adventure in the tree farm?"

Oh, baby. Let me show you.

I take her hand and start leading her toward our newest playground.

YES... BOOK TWO IS COMING...

Taken in the Tree Farm:
November 2025

Both *Pounded in the Patch* and *Taken in the Tree Farm* follow Seraphina and Luke, but will be able to be read as standalones. Obviously they're better together, but if you've got a friend looking for a spicy Christmas novella... Well, you know what to do.

I hope you've enjoyed *Pounded in the Patch*!

PREORDER ON AMAZON

ACKNOWLEDGMENTS

Street Team:

You are fucking incredible. Thank you for all you do. Words will never express how grateful I am for your time and support. You are so special to me.

ARC Team:

You signed up for this book based on spooky, slutty vibes. You are truly my kind of people. Thank you for taking a chance on me.

Rocky:

Thank you for being such a rock-solid editor. I am so appreciative of your time and dedication to making my books the best version of themselves.

Josh:

Thank you for listening to my wild, kinky ideas. And for not judging too hard when I tell you there are 9-10 orgasms in this book (yes, I lost count. were you counting???), a candy corn vibrator, a gothic sex alter, and he cuts her panties off with a knife. I also appreciate you attempting to help me find the word I'm thinking of but can't quite think of. I can't think of a single time you've actually given me the word I'm thinking of, but I do appreciate the effort and commitment.

T.C. Kraven:

Where to even start??? You literally make my world go round. You are the friend I can call at any hour of the day and I know you'll be there. Thank you for protecting me and helping me get through the hard times. (Side note, T.C. Kraven wrote **_HEADLESS HARVEST._** Go get it on Amazon right fucking now if you want to read about a witch and her lover with a pumpkin head and a gourd for a dick.)

B & B:

My babies. Thank you for encouraging me to be the best version of myself. You push me to keep going, even when it feels really hard. It's all for you. My life is for you.

Chip:

My cute-ass pomeranian. Thank you for pissing on the ground occasionally (he's only 5 months old and learning) to give me a break from editing. I know you don't do it on purpose, but I secretly enjoy the break.

ABOUT THE AUTHOR

Dana LeeAnn lives for the dark side of romance—the stalkier, the better. She writes books packed with suspense and questionable love interests that will leave your heart racing through each page turn. When she's not dreaming up new ways to torture her characters (and readers), she can be found in northern Colorado, exploring new hobbies or hiking.

[Instagram] [Facebook]

ALSO BY DANA LEEANN

The Wrecked Series (erotic horror)

Carving for Cara (1)

Little Nightmare (2)

Slaying for Sloan (3)

Sweet Doe (4) (December 2025)

The Starling Series (dark fantasy)

Crown of Blood and Stars (1)

Lady of the Lost Fae (2)

Off with Her Head (dark romance/fantasy)

Take Her to the Grave (dark paranormal romance)

Thrill of the Hunt (erotic horror)

Stream & Scream (erotic horror)

Unnamed Series (erotic horror)

Pounded in the Patch

Taken in the Tree Farm (November 2025)

Stalkers Anonymous (2026) (dark rom-com)

Printed in Dunstable, United Kingdom

70352155R00099